Freedom's Game

written by
Rosanne Tolin

Reycraft Books
145 Huguenot Street
New Rochelle, NY 10801

reycraftbooks.com

Reycraft Books is a trade imprint and trademark of Newmark Learning, LLC.

Text © 2024 by Rosanne Tolin

All rights reserved. No portion of this book may be reproduced, stored in a retrieval system, or transmitted in any form or by any means, electronic, mechanical, photocopying, recording, or otherwise, without written permission from the publisher. For information regarding permission, please contact info@reycraftbooks.com.

Educators and Librarians: Our books may be purchased in bulk for promotional, educational, or business use. Please contact sales@reycraftbooks.com.

This is a work of fiction. Names, characters, places, dialogue, and incidents described either are the product of the author's imagination or are used fictitiously.

Sale of this book without a front cover or jacket may be unauthorized. If this book is coverless, it may have been reported to the publisher as "unsold or destroyed" and may have deprived the author and publisher of payment.

Library of Congress Control Number: 2024934305

Hardcover ISBN: 978-1-4788-7619-9
Paperback ISBN: 978-1-4788-7620-5

Author photo: Courtesy of Rosanne Tolin
Photo Credits: Page iv: Danica Jovanov/Getty Images; Page v: PeterHermesFurian/Getty Images; Page viii: Dawid Kalisinski Photography/Getty Images

Printed in Dongguan, China. 8557/0624/21318
10 9 8 7 6 5 4 3 2 1

First Edition published by Reycraft Books 2024.

Reycraft Books and Newmark Learning, LLC, support diversity and the First Amendment and celebrate the right to read.

Jacket illustration by Vali Mintzi

For Mom—
I still see you everywhere.

"Where there's hope, there's life. It fills us with fresh courage and makes us strong again."

—*Anne Frank: The Diary of a Young Girl*

"Personne ne pourra détruit la culture Juive. Nobody can destroy Jewish culture."

—*Georges Loinger: New York Times,* **January 4, 2019**

1

Ziggy

September 1942

Ziggy Wirth was riding the bumpiest train in history.

He watched the trees streak by the window, an autumn palette of gold and green. He'd last seen his mother through a window like this one. Jogging, then sprinting, along the depot platform in Berlin, tears streaming down her face.

His throat tightened at the memory. What if the Gestapo had seen her at the station that day? Secret police were hunting Jewish people all over Germany.

On that trip by locomotive to Versailles—three years ago, when World War II began—Ziggy told himself he would see his parents again.

Now he knew better.

"Ziggy?" A plump face popped up over the seat in front of him.

"Yes, Greta?"

"Do you have any biscuits left?" she asked in German.

Ziggy tensed and looked around. "Can you say 'please'?" he replied in loud, deliberate French.

Greta blushed. "Oh! Thee—voo—play?"

Her lisp was more pronounced when she was nervous. Ziggy reached in his satchel for a package of buns, ignoring a twinge of guilt for making Greta uneasy. But a dozen Jewish orphans on a train speeding through Vichy France with hundreds of strangers, either supporters of Adolf Hitler or too scared for their own lives to risk helping others, couldn't afford to slip up.

Most of northern France, including Paris, was under Hitler's control. Now the Nazi party's reach was moving south. That's why Ziggy and ten other children were traveling to Annemasse, France—a new hideaway near the Swiss border. He was sure it was another temporary stay. There was no permanent home for kids like him anymore.

Before their departure, the nice people working for the secret aid society *Oeuvre de Secours Aux Enfants*—OSE for short—issued a stern warning.

"Many French people know of our efforts to help Jewish children from Austria and Germany escape," a silver-haired gentleman with a Swiss accent had explained. "Most will look the other way and pretend not to see. Do not give them reason to see."

Ziggy understood. All the older children did. But he worried about the younger ones, like Greta. How could she grasp such a threat?

The train's rattle made his teeth hurt.

He handed Greta a hard biscuit. She stuffed it in her mouth and slid down the seat. His own belly rumbled, but when he tried a dry bite, the bun made him cough. Coughing attracted attention.

"Everything okay?"

Out of nowhere, a towering stranger surfaced. He peered at Ziggy through eyes the size of robins' eggs.

Instead of staring back, Ziggy rubbed the knapsack clasp with his thumb.

"Yes, sir, we're fine."

"Then it seems I'm doing my job," the mysterious gentleman grinned. "I've been tasked with accompanying you all to Annemasse. My name is Georges Loinger. And you are?"

"Ziggy. Ziggy Wirth."

"Pleased to meet you. Not much longer to go. I need to use the latrine, would you and Felix watch the group?"

Ziggy glanced at the rail-thin boy beside him. Felix nodded.

"Yes, sir."

"Yes, sir," Ziggy echoed. Georges seemed friendly enough. But he looked so much like the German officers patrolling in Versailles.

How much longer could they hide? Knowing who to trust was impossible.

Nine years earlier, a newly elected Nazi party banned Jews from teaching in German schools. Some citizens blamed them for hardships that followed Germany losing World War I. Ziggy's father, a professor at the University of Berlin, was in danger of losing his job.

When Ziggy was in first grade, the university's dean, Herr Schneider, came to dinner. His vigorous handshake made Ziggy's arm wiggle like an overcooked noodle. The dean drew long and dramatically on his pipe before saying important things, and spoke in fragments—two or three words a puff.

"We're good friends…you and I," Herr Schneider said to Ziggy's father, like the line had been rehearsed. "We both want—*chuff puff*—what's best for the students.

"The Third Reich's ideals are our top priority," the man went on, eyes narrowing. The pipestem hung from his mouth like a door off its hinge. "It's our civic duty to restore the country's old ways—not to disrupt them. If we can agree on this, I'll assure the administration knows you're worth keeping around."

Ziggy's pa had dabbed a napkin on his forehead. "Books written by Jewish scholars, mine included, are considered un-German," was his chilly response. "They're being burned by the thousands. I'm keenly aware of the Nazis' directive."

As Herr Schneider had promised, Ziggy's pa kept his professorship until 1935, when the Nuremberg Laws stripped every German Jew of their rights. And then the unthinkable happened. When one of Pa's students snitched on him for planning a clandestine protest, the dean ratted him out to the Gestapo.

After Pa was fired, Ziggy's ma paid the rent by running an illegal bakeshop from their kitchen. She risked going to jail for making braided loaves of bread—called challah—a dozen at a time. Some were plain, brushed in shiny egg yolk; others were spotted with rye seeds or raisins. Her three-tiered cakes were decorated with meringue-rose bouquets.

Ziggy hand-delivered the boxes of pastries, holding them gingerly like a waiter carrying a tray of china. Neighbors raved about her rich confections in whispers. *The buttercream frosting! That decadent babka!*

His stomach growled again, this time at the memory of Ma's honey kuchen. He tried to silence the noise by pulling his knapsack in closer, and when Georges walked off, he turned to Felix. "Are you nervous about our new place?" he murmured, ignoring his roaring middle.

Felix shook his head, his red curls bounced like metal springs. "No. The OSE made the arrangements. They run the homes for refugees like us. We'll be fine."

For a minute, Ziggy considered spilling his doubts. But 16-year-old Felix was so sincere, so serious, so… logical. Besides, he had no proof Georges was up to anything.

Not at this moment.

He'd keep his uncertainty to himself for now.

"Where are you going, Peter?" Greta's round face appeared again. The six-year-old boy ran down the aisle in his red rubber boots, squealing wildly.

"Tag, Greta! You're it!"

Greta sprang from her seat, wisps of orange hair straying from her braids, and raced after Peter. Ziggy stood to see where they were going. His gangly body wobbled as the train car swayed. A sharp pain gripped his left leg, which was shorter and weaker than his right, thanks to a bout of polio when he was three. When he was seven, his parents bought him an expensive pair of custom-made shoes with soles that evened out the length of his legs. Now he wished he had another pair to hide his limp. He wasn't ashamed of it, but anything that might draw stares was a risk.

Some adult passengers slept. Others observed the commotion. Most of them smiled at Greta and Peter's antics. Ziggy figured their patience wouldn't last long.

Already, an elderly man with wire-rimmed glasses cast a disdainful eye at the rowdy children. He grunted and shook out his newspaper. More like he was pretending to read, Ziggy guessed, so he could spy on the person next to him. The one with all the padlocked luggage.

"To your seats now," Felix directed, taking Peter's small hand. Ziggy took Greta's, and they wound their way back. The train rocked and then screamed to a halt. Greta nearly toppled over as Georges reentered the carriage.

"I see I've put the right men in charge. Little troublemakers," he teased, ruffling Peter's brown bangs. The child's shiny eyes danced. Ziggy tried to relax.

It was hard to do when the world was filled with secrets.

Suddenly, the carriage door whooshed open. Two men wearing black leather trench coats with scarlet armbands stepped inside. Greta squeezed Ziggy's hand. The whole coach quieted.

"Good morning," one of the Nazis greeted Georges.

Ziggy's breathing stopped momentarily. "*Bonjour—*" Georges replied…

…then Greta let out an enormous sneeze.

"AH-*CHOO!*"

All eyes turned to the little girl, who clapped her hands over her mouth.

The older of the officers smiled, revealing a gold-capped front tooth.

"Gesundheit," he said.

Ziggy closed his eyes, held his breath again. He waited for Greta to answer in German.

"Mer-thee!"

French. Shocked and relieved, he opened his eyes. Greta blinked owlishly up at the guard, who snickered at her lisp. "And where are you headed this morning?" he asked.

"Annemasse," Georges hastily replied, before she could answer. "The children were discharged from an infirmary. They were traumatized by the shelling in, ah…Marseilles. Doctors prescribed a stay in the countryside."

"Hm. I see," the first guard said. "What a shame. May we insist on escorting you there?" He reached into the pocket of his uniform and produced a flat bar wrapped in silver foil. "How about a little treat first?"

He unwrapped the chocolate. Greta gasped in delight. The Nazi snapped off a chunk and handed one to her, another to Peter. When he broke off a third piece and offered it to Ziggy, he hesitated before accepting.

As much as he hated to admit it, his mouth watered. He couldn't remember the last time he'd eaten any sort of candy. He took the chocolate, popped it in his mouth, and let the sweet cocoa dissolve on his tongue.

"*Merci*," he said to the officer. But what he really wanted to do was spit chocolate right in the man's eyes.

The train car shuddered and clanged again. For the remainder of the trip, Ziggy didn't utter a word. What would happen when they reached Annemasse? What if the Nazis found out who they really were, and why they were there?

"Next stop, Annemasse."

The train jostled, then stopped, and the children tailed Georges and the soldiers onto the platform and out of the station. Even Greta and Peter, who normally chattered nonstop, hushed while Georges talked to the guards. It was more like he whispered to them.

Not to worry, I'll take care of the kids, Ziggy thought he heard him say. What exactly did that mean? He strained to hear more conversation, but the cars rumbling down the cobblestone street made it impossible.

Is Georges a secret agent for the Nazis he wondered?

In May 1938, Ziggy's pa was accused of conspiring to overthrow Hitler's government and was sent an order for immediate deportation. "You must hide at once," his father had implored. Ziggy and his ma barely had time to pack a suitcase before his father was seized.

Had Pa been double-crossed again, by another colleague? After he was fired, a handful of his former students visited him at home. Only to discuss history broadly—the Roman Empire, medieval Germany—but not current politics...as far as Ziggy knew. If their small, intellectual gatherings worried his ma, she didn't let on.

Like Pa, she always wanted to see the good in people. She dusted the oak cabinets before their guests came over, closed the living room curtains as they hung up their coats, served them warm, sticky strudel on doily napkins.

Then out of nowhere, the telegram arrived, and Pa was whisked off to a holding camp.

Would Georges betray Ziggy and the ten other children? What if he was leading them all to their doom?

They passed a courtyard where pigeons swooped for crumbs, then turned down a narrow avenue. At the end of an empty street stood a limestone building crawling with tangled vines. The sign in front read ANNEMASSE WELCOME CENTER.

The group filed inside, the fatty scent of chicken soup filling their noses. *At last*, Ziggy thought, *something to eat other than stale biscuits...*

...and a Nazi's chocolate bar dangled like fishing bait.

"Mmm," Greta moaned behind him. He fought the urge to shush her.

Down a hall corridor, two men huddled together. One in a slate-blue suit was barrel-chested and bearded, while the other, a squat man with a thick mustache, wore a French militia uniform. The material on his red trousers was so stiff, it looked like it might crack.

They looked up, then turned back toward each other.

"Commander Tremblay, thank you for stopping by," the man in the blue suit said, holding out his hand.

The militia officer gave it a firm shake. "A pleasure, as always," he replied with a curt nod. He marched past the children, his eyes straight ahead.

The blue-suited man faced them, bowing like a circus ringmaster. "Welcome, friends, welcome to Annemasse! Allow me to introduce myself," he said, taking Georges' hands in both of his own. "I am Mayor Jean Deffaugt, and I'm thrilled you're here. I trust your journey was pleasant?"

"It was, thank you," Georges said. "Though the little ones got a bit rambunctious."

The mayor chuckled. "Understandable, of course. It's a long ride. We've prepared a late supper for you all—and of course, you gentlemen are welcome to join us."

This last bit was directed to the trench coats.

"A kind offer, but we have other business to attend to," one guard said.

"*Au revoir*, children. Enjoy your time here," the other added smugly. A few kids mumbled *merci*. Most only shuffled their feet as the soldiers strode off.

Mayor Deffaugt motioned to the children. He led them past a sign that read EXIT FOR CAMPERS ONLY. They entered a dining hall, where tables overflowed with bowls of salty broth and slabs of gruyere cheese.

Though the food was delicious, and Ziggy was starving, he couldn't manage to eat much. He emptied half of his soup bowl into Greta's and Peter's. As they chatted and slurped, Ziggy worried. Already, Nazis had seen them here—no, they'd escorted them. How long could they keep up the pretense of being French children, here to regain their health?

Back home in Berlin, Nazis relentlessly rounded up Jews. And at Maison du Mouton, his orphanage in Versailles—there'd been talk of soldiers pillaging Jewish homes. Ziggy pretended to stir his broth, trying not to think of the last time he'd seen his father, or the reason why his mother had never written.

How long could *this* chateau keep them safe? A week? A month? A year?

He braced himself for the worst. Sooner or later, the worst was bound to happen.

2

Elka

Twelve-year-old Elka woke up sweating in twisted sheets. Strands of chestnut hair stuck to her cheeks like wet leaves.

In her dream, she'd soared like a falcon through a midnight forest. A clawed beast with ragged breath trailed her. Thorny tree limbs arched like fingernails, blocking her view of the ground below.

Elka threw off her wool blanket. Sunlight streamed through the dormitory window onto four rows of empty bunk beds. She'd slept in! She never slept in. Frantic, Elka leaped out of bed, dressed briskly and pulled on her ankle-high boots. No time for breakfast—she'd have to wait for lunch and hope her stomach didn't growl during lessons.

She raced out of the chateau and veered right on Avenue Florissant. The street was lined with oak trees, and Elka took a good, long breath as she ran, savoring their smoky smell. Scarlet-lobed leaves hid among the gold ones. A few littered the path like confetti. This would be her third fall in Annemasse. Three years since she'd seen her family. Three years since her world—the *whole* world, it seemed—had turned upside down.

Goosebumps sprinkled her arms, but she didn't turn back for a sweater. No time!

The police were out for morning patrol in bigger numbers. Normally, Elka traveled to school with a flock of kids like herself—Jewish but pretending not to be. Being alone felt especially perilous.

She slowed to a swift walk, should an officer stroll by…

…and spotted three men in mud-colored uniforms. She skidded to a halt.

Don't let them see. Don't let them see. The words beat a rhythm in her mind. Elka darted behind a tree and waited ten long seconds before peering around the trunk. A block ahead, the men turned onto another street. She abandoned her hideout and jogged the rest of the way.

She sighed with relief when she saw the timber schoolhouse. A bunch of children, from kindergartners to eighth form, still mingled in the courtyard. She wasn't that late.

"El-ka!" came a singsong voice. She fixed her hazel eyes on the latched door, disregarding the snickers. In her peripheral vision, she could see a clique of girls in blue and gray smocks. Jeannine Tremblay called out again, louder this time.

"*El*-ka!"

Again, she ignored her. Jeannine wasn't worth listening to. A pretty, pixie-like girl with a sharp tongue, Jeannine had been more insufferable than usual, ever since her father was promoted to commander of a volunteer militia last spring. Jeannine thought that made her the commander of the whole school.

Elka unlatched the door and rushed inside, the laughter fading behind her.

The school was modest in size. Two classrooms, both perfectly square. But with sixty students, half of them orphans—it was full to bursting. Sitting cross-legged on the floor made it tough to concentrate. That was one reason Elka liked coming early.

The biggest reason was spending time with her teacher.

"*Bon matin!*"

Mademoiselle Bellegard smiled at her. A short woman with shiny hair the color of honey, her teacher had the most stick-straight posture she'd ever seen. Mama had forever been correcting Elka's posture, gently lifting her narrow chin with one finger and pressing softly between her shoulder blades. Even with those reminders, she slouched a minute later.

"*Bonjour,* Mademoiselle." After three years of practice, her French sounded natural. That's what her teacher said, anyhow. But no matter how hard Elka tried, Jeannine claimed she could still hear her native German accent.

"Our morning exercise," Mademoiselle gestured toward the chalkboard, where she'd listed ten verbs in her graceful script. Across the top were pronouns: *je, tu, il/elle, nous, vous.*

Verb conjugations were Elka's least favorite. She stifled a groan, pulling a grainy pebble from her too-tight shoe. Another hole was starting on the knee of her stocking.

Elka studied the first verb. She let it simmer in her mind, before reading aloud.

"*Recueillir,*" she said slowly.

"*Bien!*" Mademoiselle encouraged. "Present tense first."

Chalk in hand, Elka wrote each verb in all its forms while Mademoiselle settled a quarrel in the corner of the room. When Elka made a slight mistake, she wiped it away with a wool eraser. Soon Mademoiselle came back to check on her. She cupped a warm hand over Elka's and together, they traced her teacher's perfect loops.

Being the teacher's pet wasn't something she'd been used to. Growing up in Dresden, she was scolded for racing boys at recess. When she got mud stains on her skirt, she was sent to the washroom while the other students started lessons.

That was then. Now, mastering French wasn't only about getting good grades—it meant being unnoticeable, not sounding foreign. Someday her life might depend on it. Jeannine and the other girls in the courtyard would never understand that.

After finishing her conjugations, Elka tiptoed over the pine planks to an empty spot. Careful not to step on her classmates' fingers, she sank cross-legged onto the floor.

"Hi, Elka." Hettie, a girl from the chateau one year younger, plunked down to her right.

Jeannine and her friend Romilly strolled in next. Jeannine surveyed the room, her lip curled in a sneer.

"Mademoiselle Bellegard," she said loudly for the whole class to hear. "My father isn't going to be happy if he hears I had to sit on the floor again."

Elka bit her tongue to keep from snapping back. She'd made that error before and paid for it. Best to let her teacher, who welcomed everyone, handle it.

Mademoiselle's smile tightened. "Now, Jeannine. No one, including you, has ever sat on the floor all day. As always, we'll shuffle around after lunch."

Rolling her ice-blue eyes, Jeannine stomped to a space by Elka. As she sat, their shoulders brushed, and Jeannine recoiled like she'd touched a hot flame. Elka flushed with shame. Which was ridiculous, she told herself.

Jeannine waited until Mademoiselle was busy pulling out her roll book before huffing to Romilly, "I don't think it's fair, considering this is supposed to be a good Christian school." On the other side of Elka, Hettie stared at her hands. Elka pressed her lips together so hard it hurt.

"A good school is a good school, Jeannine," Mademoiselle said, straightening up. Her tone was light, but Elka noticed a steeliness in her gaze. "It can only make the world a better place. Your classmates have been prescribed fresh air and safe shelter. Surely you agree everyone deserves an education, even if the schoolhouse is a little cramped—yes?"

Elka's love for her teacher was cemented. Especially when Jeannine's cheeks reddened, and she ducked her head.

"Yes, Mademoiselle," she muttered.

But she made a face as soon as her teacher's back was turned, then leaned over to whisper in Romilly's ear. This time, Elka couldn't hear what she said. But the glare Jeannine shot her afterwards sent a shiver up her spine that had nothing to do with the chill outside.

After morning recess, Elka cornered her teacher. "Mademoiselle, I'm sorry I forgot my homework. I woke up late and I…"

Her apology evaporated. An older boy she'd never seen before stood in front of the class. His rumpled red locks made him look like he'd been struck by a lightning bolt.

"Elka," Mademoiselle Bellegard smiled. "No apologies necessary—bring it with you tomorrow. Now please take a seat, we have two new students with us today."

Elka could feel Jeannine's scowl.

Mademoiselle turned to the messy-haired boy. "Thank you for introducing yourself, Felix. If there's nothing more you'd like to share, you may be seated. Ziggy, will you please come join me?"

Surprised, Elka saw another new boy. He looked close to her age, with brown hair long enough to spiral at the ends. His eyes were soft and serious, like he knew things no one his age should.

The boy swung out his right leg and rose from his seat. He leaned left, palming the desk for support. She wondered what sort of injury he had. Maybe he'd broken his femur, like she had five winters ago, skating on an icy pond, pretending to be Sonja Henie. When she attempted an axel, she lost her balance and smacked the frozen surface.

The memory of her painful fall wasn't so bad. Papa had made her feel better. He warmed a mug of cider when the doctor came to set her leg in a cast. Elka remembered her impatience waiting for the steaming drink to cool so she wouldn't burn her tongue. To pass time while she healed, Papa taught her to pick a lock with a hairpin. Mama frowned, suggesting a tame game of checkers instead.

For three whole weeks, Elka walked with crutches. Her armpits ached, and her palms blistered from gripping the wooden bars. When her parents weren't home, she hobbled around the house without them—a big mistake. She'd been mad as a hornet when the doctor made her wear the cast an extra two weeks.

But there weren't crutches next to Ziggy.

"I'm from Berlin, but I've been living in France for a while."

Jeannine, who sat just below the new boy, stretched her arms wide. Her hand swiped his leg with a thwack.

"Even—excuse me." He tripped and caught himself on the desk. "Even before that, I'd traveled here some. My aunt went to boarding school in Paris and married a Frenchman, so my parents and I visited her on holiday." Ziggy glanced at a stack of books on Mademoiselle's desk. "I used to spend summers reading in her bookstore there, at 36 Rue de Bucherie."

"How lovely," Mademoiselle cooed. Elka could tell her teacher was as impressed with Ziggy's perfect French as she was. "What was it like?"

His pale face brightened. "Wonderful! The shelves were made of cherry wood. They reached all the way to the ceiling. There was a ladder you climbed to reach the rare history volumes on top. My aunt collected old books. They smelled like a mix of musk and coffee…"

Jeannine yawned dramatically, as though all this talk of books was boring her. Ziggy saw her glazed look and got quiet. Elka silently willed him to continue. The bookstore sounded magical. Even the address, *36 Rue de Bucherie*, had her spellbound. When he described it, she felt transported there.

Maybe Ziggy thought he'd shared too much.

"It was very nice," he finished, then sat back down.

Mademoiselle clapped her hands. "It sounds positively divine. Okay, class, shall we begin? *Sortez vos compositions…*"

Elka couldn't focus the rest of the morning. Between sleeping in, hiding behind the tree from the police, conceited Jeannine, and the excitement of two brand-new students, she was wound up like a ball of string. When Mademoiselle dismissed class for lunch, she shot to her feet and hurried over to Ziggy.

She lingered while he collected his things, unsure what to say. Clutching the back of his chair, Ziggy turned with a small hop—and spooked when he saw her.

"Oh, sorry," he said. "Am I in your way? I move kind of slowly. Thanks to this." He tapped his left leg. It was skinnier than his right.

"No, no, it's not that at all." Now she was the flustered one. "I just…um…wanted to introduce myself. I'm Elka."

"Oh." Ziggy tossed a pencil in his knapsack. "Nice to meet you."

"I also wanted to—to apologize for Jeannine. I promise we're not all…um, like *her*. Your aunt's bookstore sounds incredible. I've never been to Paris. I'm from Germany too, like you—Dresden, have you been there?—but I've lived here for almost four years. Everyone at the chateau is really nice—Monsieur Francois is in charge of running things. Have you met Darcy? She's the cook; she's so funny. Speaking of Darcy, we should get lunch. Are you hungry? I'm starving."

Elka knew she was talking too much. She couldn't stop herself. Whether it was the thrill of new classmates or the extra hours of sleep, she wasn't sure.

"You go ahead." Ziggy slung his bag on a shoulder. "I'll slow you down."

Was he annoyed by her rambling? Elka twirled her long ponytail. "It's no problem. Tell me more about the bookstore. I mean, that is, if you don't mind."

They walked side-by-side to the chateau and sat together in the dining hall. Elka gnawed a baguette while Ziggy told her how his father was a history professor. He'd grown up in a house practically furnished with books, and he *loved* reading. To Elka, it seemed like he was on a mission to read every single book in the world.

"I don't usually talk about myself that much." He tore off a crust of bread and examined it. "Our old cook added sawdust to the flour, too. Makes it go farther, I guess. Anyways, how about you? Tell me more about Dresden?"

While he bit into the roll, Elka cleared her throat. "What do you want to know?" Then a flash of fair hair whisked by. "Wait. Who is that man?"

Ziggy stopped chewing. When Elka waved a hand to get his attention, he seemed distracted, so she dropped it. "Let me see. For starters, I was the fastest runner in third form." When the worst insult she ever heard was "tomboy." When she went home every day to her family, instead of an orphanage.

She sucked in her breath. Was this boy even listening? He'd seemed nice at first, but now he was acting rude.

She turned her head to where Felix sat a table over, with his nose in a book. "He seems awfully quiet."

Ziggy snapped out of his trance. "He is—sometimes. Smart, too. His father was a captain in the last war. He was considered for an Iron Cross. Not many Jews were awarded military honors, you know."

"Wow," she whispered. She knew German Jews were no longer welcome in Hitler's army. Besides, who would want to fight for their enemy?

Then the unfamiliar man walked by, with the flat-topped blond hair. "Tell me, please. Who is *he*?"

Ziggy rubbed the back of his neck. "That's Georges."

"Who?"

"Wish I knew exactly. I'm not sure. All I know is his name is Georges—Georges Loinger. He rode the train from Versailles with us." Ziggy lowered his voice. "He says he works for the OSE."

Elka relaxed. She knew about the OSE. Most of them did. The man was square shouldered like her Papa, with an easy smile and eyes the color of cornflowers. "How long is he staying here?"

Ziggy shrugged. "No idea."

His shallow answer irked her. "What is it?"

"What do you mean? What is what?"

"I mean there's more you're not saying." She fixed Ziggy with her best *don't you dare lie to me face*. "So... say it."

"I think he might be a spy."

Elka felt a flicker of excitement, quickly followed by disbelief. "Wait—a spy for who?"

Ziggy shrugged again. "That's what I'm saying. Maybe Nazis? I don't know."

Before Elka could respond, Monsieur Francois's voice boomed. "Listen up, children. I have something important to tell you."

Elka set her baguette down. Today was full of unusual news.

"Monsieur Loinger, whom some of you newcomers met on the train ride here, isn't solely your chaperone. From now on, he will also be your gym teacher."

Huh? Was she hearing that right? A *gym* teacher?

Ziggy knitted his eyebrows. Elka smirked. *A gym teacher!* If Georges was here to teach gym class, that meant they could trust him, right?

The way he carried himself made her feel protected. Of course, a good, confident spy could fool anyone.

And Georges had blue eyes and straw-colored hair, like so many Nazi soldiers.

Elka shook off her darker thoughts.

She would prove Ziggy wrong. Georges was no spy!

3

Ziggy

Maison du Mouton had been smaller, brighter—but the heart of Chateau Annemasse beat in its drawing room. Paintings of aristocratic picnics hung in fading gilt frames. An enormous stone hearth cast heat wall-to-wall.

If you looked past chipping paint, and fat rats, it appeared a nice enough place to live. For forty kids with missing parents at least. Anyhow, Elka seemed happy here. That is, apart from being busy with chores (today she was on laundry duty, her least favorite, she said—"the boys' socks stink something dreadful"). She lit up around Monsieur Francois, Darcy the cook, and most of all, Mademoiselle Bellegard.

But she hadn't spoken of her mother or father. Things had been the same at the safe house in Versailles. They didn't share what happened to their families because none of the kids knew for sure. If their parents and siblings weren't in hiding...well, the rumors were too sinister to bear. The children shut them down like trapdoors.

It was a bright June morning four years ago, when Ziggy was awakened by the sound of the doorbell. When he opened the door, the neighborhood postman stood, rigid as a toy soldier. "*Guten Morgen*," the man said, handing Ziggy a sealed envelope addressed to his father.

Ziggy rubbed the sleep from his eyes. "*Guten Morgen*, Herr Schmidt."

The mailman saluted and then turned on his heel. Ziggy quickly shut the door, then hop-skipped to the bathroom where his mother washed socks in the marble basin. He showed her the piece of mail. She dried her hands on a damp rag and fell silent.

When she finally spoke, her voice shook. "Take your bike to the store...for, eh—for eggs. There is money in the coin jar. Go on now!"

Confused, Ziggy obeyed his mother. But his insides burned like when he ate second helpings of sauerkraut with mustard cream sauce. Her insistence on the errand was strange. War rationing meant a dairy shortage; store shelves would be nearly empty. Besides, his parents complained about the price of groceries.

"I remember ten years ago, when a barrel of Reichsmarks bought a single pint of milk," his ma would scold when he begged for Riesen candies. "The pantry was always bare, but we managed."

That night, while reading a *Tintin* comic for the hundredth time, Ziggy overheard his parents' conversation. They whispered somberly about sending him out of Berlin. His parents talked of "deportations," where thousands of Jews were rounded up and forced to live in horrible conditions, confined in crowded ghettos—or worse, in prison-like concentration camps.

His aunt had even offered to send him to the United States. At the time, the idea seemed crazy to Ziggy. What place was safer than home?

That evening—before the Nazis arrested Ziggy's father, before Ziggy was told the envelope had contained a call-up for his father to a camp—he and his ma disappeared overnight. They hid four-doors-down in Frau Wagner's attic, where heavy black screens on the windows shrouded the sunlight. Grownups didn't discuss the dangers of being seen. By then, Ziggy didn't need them to. There were plenty of clues. He could read the sign outside:

SPIES ARE EVERYWHERE. SEE SOMETHING, SAY SOMETHING.

There, in the neighbor's attic, the air clung to Ziggy like a thick, weighty mist. Time indoors was tense and glum. On a pitch-black November night, five months after his father's arrest, he was roused by a chain of rapid-fire pops. Scanning the room with a flashlight, he saw his mother sitting upright in a paper-thin nightgown, her hollow face as white as paste.

Desperate cries for help rose from the street below.

Please don't take him away, sir!

Followed by a chorus of sobs, stamped out by the brutish orders of Hitler's Stormtroopers. Ash floated through the window cracks, like black snowflakes. Ziggy put his fingers in his ears, squeezed his eyes closed. Hot, smoky soot stung the back of his throat.

When he finally opened his eyes, his ma stood near him. A mug of water cupped between her hands. She held it out. He covered a cough, shook his head.

"I drank yesterday's, remember? You need it more." Outside the apartment, the yelling and the smashing of glass subsided, but a few dogs still bayed and growled.

After the brutal attack, life in the attic grew even darker, quieter. That violent night became known as *Kristallnacht*—the Night of the Broken Glass. Throughout Germany, Jews' homes and shops were destroyed, and temples were burned to the ground. Then three months later, Frau Wagner found a letter from Pa in her mail slot. She set it on Ziggy's nightstand, with a bowl of cold broth.

The return address was Dachau, Germany.

Thirty of us arrived on a train car meant to move cattle. On better days I'm brick laying or concrete stamping. It is dull work, but I listen to the whistling wrens. Pa had written with his usual positivity. *Have faith the hard times will end.*

Halevai—I wish it were so.

I love you, son.

After eight months in hiding, Ziggy knew the truth.

Home wasn't safe. Nowhere was safe.

So, when his mother arranged shelter for him in northern France, he didn't argue. It wasn't crazy. It was the best chance he had to survive.

Ziggy rinsed off a plate and swallowed the lump in his throat.

"Seems decent here, don't you think?" He handed the plate to Felix, who dried it absentmindedly.

"It does. I used my duffle as a pillow last night, but at least my bed's longer in this place. Now I can sleep without my feet hanging over the edge."

Ziggy laughed. "School was okay, too. The teacher's nice."

"She is." While Felix quietly dried another dish, Ziggy recalled his mother saying his father was a "thinker." She meant it as a compliment. She said just because he didn't talk much, didn't mean he had nothing to say. Felix was the same way. Days after Hitler rose to power, he came home from school and his dad was gone.

"The classroom's packed," said Felix. "Not everyone's happy about our arrival."

Ziggy knew who he meant. The girl that yawned when he described his aunt's bookstore. She'd glared daggers when they'd entered the schoolhouse.

"I guess I can't blame them," Ziggy said. "They have to sit on the floor because of us."

Felix wrung the towel and brown liquid trickled into the sink. "I suspect some of them are put off about more than not having a desk."

Ziggy's gut twanged like a guitar string. His friend was right.

"Do you remember that man at the Welcome Center? The one talking to the mayor?"

"The commander?" Ziggy pictured the stout, whiskered man wearing a militia uniform. "What about him?"

"Commander *Tremblay*." Felix arched an eyebrow. "I asked around. He's Jeannine's dad. Turns out he's in step with the Nazis."

A cold pit wrenched Ziggy's inside.

"Are you two almost finished?"

Both boys turned to see Elka, hands on her hips, standing in the entryway. She wore a threadbare wool romper and worn leather boots.

"Almost." Ziggy turned off the spigot. "Where are you going?"

"Gym." Elka yanked her ponytail. "Darcy, are you… wait—where's Darcy?"

The cook poked her head out of the freezer. "Back here, turning into an ice pop."

Yesterday, Darcy ran gym class. Elka and the other children fell over themselves when she keeled over after ten jumping jacks.

Elka smiled. "Are you leading class again this afternoon?"

"Not today, dear. Your new instructor is taking over." She gave the kids a wave before disappearing back inside the ice chest.

"Aw," Elka frowned. "Darcy's my favorite gym teacher. Come on, let's go!"

She took off without waiting for the boys. "That girl really likes it here." Felix piled the clean plates on a lopsided shelf. "I suppose that's a good sign."

Ziggy wasn't so sure. Truthfully, he couldn't decide whether he admired or resented her enthusiasm. He, too, longed to feel secure. To only worry about things like who was teaching gym that day. But how could he know they were safe, when their new teacher had arrived, unplanned? They didn't know him. Wasn't Elka being naive?

He and Felix trailed her down the corridor, where sunbeams filtered in gold dust clouds. Outside the window, a tall man in a white T-shirt caught Ziggy's eye. Georges! His back was against the woodshed, almost hidden from view, head tilted to one side. Within earshot, two men in striped ties exchanged papers.

The scene put Ziggy on high alert. If Georges was listening to their conversation, he might be a spy. But was he a spy *for* the OSE…or was he spying on them?

He was about to tell Elka their teacher was eavesdropping when Greta raced up. Her cheeks were flushed, a purple bow dangling from her tangled hair.

Peter was right on her heels, swinging something grayish and wriggling.

"Whoa!" Felix exclaimed. Elka dodged out of Peter's way. Like a cat catching a mouse, Felix snatched Peter around the waist and scooped him up. The boy's legs pumped like he was running. Everyone watching started to laugh.

Felix spun Peter as fast as a top. "What's that you have there?"

"It's a *snake*!" Greta cried, trying hard to sound dramatic. She hid behind Ziggy.

"It's just a *worm*," Peter insisted. He held out the serpent-like creature.

"It *is* just a worm," Felix said. "But a very *big* one. And what were you doing with it?"

"He was trying to throw it in my hair!" Greta peeked around Ziggy. He tried to keep a straight face. Peter thrust the squirming worm at his small friend.

"I was not! I was trying to give it to you! It's a present!"

He stuck his fist out again. Greta shrieked.

"A little piece of advice, Peter," Felix said as he gently put the boy down. "Worms don't make great presents for girls."

"I'll take it," Elka held out her hands. Peter laid the slimy worm in her palms. "Let's go put him back, okay?"

"Okay," he agreed, and followed Elka to the garden.

Greta ran after them like a wild pony. "Hey, that was my present!" she hollered.

Felix directed the rest of the kids outdoors while Ziggy corralled the remaining stragglers. After hours in a muggy kitchen, the cool breeze was a sweet relief. Ziggy remembered Felix arriving at Maison du Mouton more than two years ago—a bony, solemn boy, with arms longer than Ziggy's legs. Now he'd grown to be the unofficial father of the group, making sense of things when Ziggy and the others couldn't.

He blinked away the old memory. Maybe living in Annemasse would be easier now that he finally knew and understood the rules. *Wear a gold cross pendant. Memorize the hymnbook.* Be someone you are not. He'd almost grown accustomed to hiding in plain sight; it felt as normal to him as such a thing ever could.

With Felix leading the way, they walked to a sloped field below the chateau. A sparkling mountain range, jagged and white, sprang up ahead of them to the north. It etched along the blue sky, beckoning them onward.

Switzerland.

When Ziggy ran out of books to read in Versailles, which hadn't taken long, he'd studied the endless tourist maps he'd found there. He knew Annemasse was just an afternoon's hike from Geneva, Switzerland, where the Nazis held no power. But as close as Geneva was, the border crossings were always fiercely guarded. On the other side was freedom, yet it was so, so far away.

"The worm made it home safely." Elka appeared at Ziggy's side and rubbed her muddy hands on her romper. "Now Peter's daring Greta to eat a turnip he dug up."

Ziggy smiled. "Those two are always getting into mischief." However, his mind remained focused on Georges listening in on the men.

"They're so funny," she said, raising her arms overhead. "I hope the new gym teacher doesn't make us do jumping jacks and push-ups. That's what Monsieur Francois does. Jumping jacks and push-ups, over and over again until—"

He cut her off, unable to hold in his skepticism. "Did you see Georges back there, by the woodshed? He was snooping, I'm sure of it. That's what I'm trying to tell you, he could be a decoy or a—"

"Listen up, class!"

Ziggy and Elka jumped to face their gym teacher and the rest of the children rushed over.

Georges—in shorts, a jersey, and bright white sneakers—motioned everyone into a circle. A whistle hung from a lanyard around his neck. Elka's face brightened, but Ziggy crossed his arms and frowned slightly.

"Good afternoon," Georges sang out in a friendly voice. "For those of you who don't know me, my name is Georges Loinger, and I'm your new gym teacher."

Well, is that so? Ziggy mused suspiciously.

"I understand gym class has been a bit...unstructured as of late, but that is all about to change. In fact, I have a big announcement."

Greta bounced on her toes, still gripping the turnip root behind her back. Georges clasped his hands together, and the group quieted.

"This spring, we're going to have a Sports Festival." Several kids let out squeals of delight. "There will be all kinds of events—a three-legged race, a sack race, a wheelbarrow race—"

"Ooh, can we have an egg and spoon race?" Peter cried. "Please? I'm so good at that!"

Georges held up a hand to calm the excited children. "Certainly, we can, and we'll also hold Olympic-style competitions, like a 400-meter sprint. If any of you have run the track, that means one lap around."

A festival? Nothing about this seemed right; in fact, it seemed downright strange.

Next to Ziggy, Elka stood motionless. He feared that she was totally falling for it, falling under this charming teacher's spell.

"We will train very hard," Georges went on. "While the festival will be a chance for each of you to show off your fitness, what sports are really about is teamwork. Which is why we'll also be forming a fully equipped soccer team."

A chorus of hoots followed. Ziggy rocked back on his heels. He wasn't good at tag, but soccer was another story. Years of relying on his good right leg had made it stronger than his left. He could send a ball all the way downfield with one kick, like a fighter delivering a knock-out punch.

Playing soccer was like a chess match—all bound up in strategy. Checkmate, he could hear his father tease, trapping Ziggy's king. The hours they'd spent trading pawns and capturing castles had taught Ziggy to anticipate his opponent's next move, and the one after that. On the soccer pitch, he could read his rival by watching the angle of his foot on the ball, or the direction her hips pivoted before attempting a breakaway.

But his soccer career had been cut short when a new round of antisemitic rules had been passed in 1937, forcing him to transfer to an all-Jewish school, where sports were strictly forbidden. Ziggy may not have been the fastest, but at least at his old school, friends had clamored to have him on their team.

Ziggy watched Georges work with the young children—who already adored him—on their ball-handling skills. Maybe Georges thought a sports festival would help boost their spirits? Or was he trying to distract everyone from his real business?

None of it really made sense. The chateau didn't have enough blankets and pillows for every child, let alone sneakers and extra soccer balls, and war rationing was only getting harsher and harsher. With each passing winter there was less food on their plates. So where was the sense in training so hard on empty stomachs?

Didn't a festival require time to arrange, to organize? The kids had schoolwork to do every night, plus every chore imaginable. Wouldn't time spent planning the festival interfere with kitchen duty and dusting and cleaning the dormitories? And how had Georges convinced Monsieur Francois to agree to this? Could it really be for the fun of it? Or was organizing something so huge, something that required them all to participate, part of a complex ruse to turn them in?

Before Ziggy had a chance to say anything to Elka about all this, Georges blew his whistle. The children snapped to orderly attention, and Georges divided them into smaller groups.

"First runner from each group, step up. Don't be shy, now!"

Elka bound out like a rabbit from a bush and jogged impatiently in place. Peter, Hettie, and two other kids hopped forward as well.

"On my whistle!" Georges called. "To the big oak tree and back. One, two—"

The five runners took off. Ziggy watched Elka fly across the field, pigtail streaming behind her. In seconds, she pulled ahead. She reached the tree, slapped it, and raced back, passing some of the others who weren't even at the halfway point yet.

"Wow," Felix mouthed.– All the others were speechless.

Including Ziggy. His eyes bugged out. Elka was fast—*very* fast. But it was the look on her face that captivated him. She was glowing—like this was her birthday party and she'd just opened the best gift ever. For a moment, his frustration over the Georges situation cooled off a bit.

The next group of runners assembled. Georges high-fived Elka as she crossed the finish line first and tagged Felix for his round of the relay race. "This is amazing!" Elka gasped, leaning over, hands on her knees, struggling to catch her breath. "Isn't it?"

Ziggy forced a polite smile. His reluctance to agree had nothing to do with his weaker leg, something he knew he made up for in ways that didn't rely on strength and speed. It was fun, and maybe he was too distrusting. Maybe Georges and Francois simply wanted to do something nice for the children. At least they'd have a special event to look forward to, and these days special events were few and far between.

But, still, Ziggy couldn't help suspecting there was more to Georges and his festival than met the eye. And Elka had to understand that, had to be made to understand it...before it was too late.

4

Elka

In primary school, Elka's running earned her more ridicule than respect. Not that she cared. She loved charging past the boys in her long cotton skirt with the bow in the back, the silk ribbons Mama tied in her hair unraveling like yarn. Even when they slipped off, into the dirt, Elka strode on.

Mama threatened a spanking every time she saw those soiled ribbons.

But she never followed through.

Papa was proud of her. He said Elka had a thick skin about the teasing. If she was Papa's favorite, then Ruth was Mama's. Unlike Elka, Ruth liked sewing frocks more than catching frogs. While Mama worked the Singer machine, Ruth embroidered tiny birds on crepe fabric. At six, she could cross stitch faster than the women at synagogue.

Elka never cared for sewing. She once heard her parents arguing about her.

"She'll have to learn to be a lady sooner or later," Mama said, punching a lump of dough. "Isn't it better to start now?"

"The world's changing, *mein liba*," Papa replied affectionately like he did when he debated Mama. "Women are taking on the work of men, thanks to rumors of war. Elka has her own mind. She'll be prepared for what's coming—mentally and physically."

At the mention of war, Elka's good mood turned to fear.

She didn't want to fight. She wanted to *run*.

As much as Papa defended what the headmistress called her "feisty behavior," he was surprised when she joined the athletic club. Mama insisted she also take piano lessons. Sitting on a hard bench practicing scales made Elka want to jump out of her skin. Still, she went along with it, so she'd be allowed to keep running.

Mama made a special bonnet for her, to keep from getting sunburned. When Elka ran the trails with her teammates, mostly boys older than herself, she untied it. She tucked it into the band of her skirt, letting the sun's rays freckle her face.

While the other girls sang choir, she traversed emerald valleys, carrying heavy canteen packs to strengthen her legs. As she trained more, she saw less and less of her girlfriends. They didn't understand what drove her to run, and she couldn't put it into words. Eventually those friends drifted away. It was just as well. When they joined the Band of German Maidens, the female Hitler youth group, it didn't hurt as much.

For almost four years, Elka smothered her running ambitions. But with Georges Loinger's arrival, the Sports Festival, the idea of a glorious relay race... everything came rushing back. As she sprinted across the grass, her dream of winning world medals was more alive than ever.

"You're blazing fast," Ziggy said during dinner. "The fastest kid here, except Felix."

Elka didn't want to brag in front of the brand-new boy. Besides, he was skeptical of everything. Paranoid even. He didn't believe Georges was a gym teacher, so why would he care about their game day anyhow. "I used to be good," was all she said.

Part of her wondered, could she beat even Felix, by training like she used to? But in the farthest crevice of her mind, for reasons she didn't dare say aloud, she felt shame for wanting to run again.

No. She didn't want to run. Not anymore.

Over the next two months, Elka settled into a new routine.

It turned out Ziggy was an early riser, too. Because of his limp, he liked to leave for school in plenty of time. Now she had someone to walk with in the mornings. He listened to her chatter, even if he didn't talk as much. While she worked through French lessons on the chalkboard, he warmed his toes by the classroom's wood-burning stove—the best spot in colder months—and read whatever book Mademoiselle Bellegard brought that day.

"Have you finished it yet?" Elka teased each time Ziggy opened a new one. He would ignore her and turn the page.

"I can see I'll have to borrow more books," Mademoiselle winked.

In the courtyard on their way from class, Jeannine taunted them. "Well, aren't you two sweet. Too bad my father says you're not wanted here anymore."

Elka fumed. The words stung like open wounds. But she was glad to have Ziggy with her, to avoid Jeannine's jeers.

"Can we slow down a little?" Steam puffed from Ziggy's mouth. The wind's mossy smell meant sleet was coming.

"I'm sorry." In her haste to leave, Elka hadn't realized she'd rushed ahead. She stopped and hugged her arms to her chest. "Does the cold make your leg hurt worse?"

Mademoiselle Bellegard had told her that Ziggy contracted polio as a little boy. After he fell ill, his legs grew different lengths.

He shook his head. "No. But it'll be slippery, playing in this weather."

Without the right shoes, his gait was uneven. But Elka noticed he never complained.

Today Georges had promised they'd learn new soccer plays. After seeing her speed weeks before, he'd put her at striker—a scoring position. Scrimmages were exciting and yet, the elation she felt after the relay filled her with guilt. Besides, Ziggy doubted the games would actually happen.

She liked his company plenty. But she was tired of his suspicion of Georges.

Other things concerned her much more. Kitchen duty came before gym—lunch had been stew with boiled cabbage again. Elka noticed the pieces of meat were punier than ever.

She mentioned this to Hettie as the two of them scrubbed pans.

"David said he doesn't think it's even beef anymore," Hettie said with a giggle, wiping sweat from her brow. "Just severely bruised potatoes. Poor souls!"

Elka laughed, though her stomach grumbled with hunger. The portions were dwindling; her bowl had been half-filled with soup. But it was hard to be picky about stew when so many Jews were suffering far worse fates.

"Jeannine was in a real mood this morning, wasn't she?" Hettie said.

"Jeannine's *always* in a mood." Elka sponged harder. Her knuckles were raw from the vinegar mixed with scalding water.

"I overheard her talking to Romilly and Celeste after class. She said she's asking her father to lodge a complaint with the school about…overcrowding."

Hettie paused before *overcrowding*. Elka knew why. Jeannine's real complaint wasn't that the school had too many students. It was that the school had students who weren't like her.

"Mademoiselle will handle it," Elka reassured her. "She always does."

She believed it. She had to. She wasn't ignorant—she saw the newspapers delivered to the chateau. During her years here she'd read headlines about Hitler's rising power, the Nazis' invasion of Poland, the fall of Paris, the Americans entering the war.

Last July, French police had mass arrested thousands of Jewish people. That had been an especially terrible time. Elka heard the moans and sobs of her bunkmates every night for a week, including Hettie.

She hadn't cried. She hardly did anymore. Sometimes she felt she had nearly four years' worth of tears and screams and rage all crammed into a tight little ball in the center of her chest, and one day it would just *explode*.

"But Jeannine's father is a legion boss now," Hettie said, handing Elka a dirty pan. "What if Mademoiselle has to listen to him?"

Elka waved a hand, greasy water dripped on her blouse. "If he's a commander, he's got bigger things to worry about than Jeannine sitting on the floor during algebra," she told Hettie, who looked relieved.

"You think so?"

"Of course!" She gave her friend a weak smile. "Don't worry, Hettie. We're safe."

Elka hurriedly wiped down the tables, then met Ziggy and Felix in the common room. Because of the rain, inside the place was a ruckus—the younger children played tag, only it wasn't clear who was "it."

Soon the sun played hide-and-seek, and a hazy rainbow spanned the mountains. *Allez vous!* Felix said and just like that, every kid fell into line like he was the Pied Piper of Hamlin. They marched to the lawn, where they were met by Monsieur Francois. The man's suspenders bowed over his waistline.

"Good afternoon, children," he said, his mustache inching up and down like a caterpillar. "Do you know why soccer players do well in school? Because they use their heads!"

The older children groaned, the little ones clutched their middles and giggled. Elka was less amused. She liked Francois well enough—just not for leading gym class.

"Where's Georges?" she whispered to Ziggy, standing on her tiptoes, searching the landscape. "He missed last Wednesday, too. And two Mondays before that."

He shrugged. She noticed he'd been sulky today. At first, she told herself it was because of his leg. But he pushed himself harder than most of the kids. Plus, he never minded coming in last. Maybe she'd been wrong about that.

This was soccer. Running and passing and kicking were different than push-ups and stretching. She wondered whether he might need to sit out.

Maybe she would sit out with him.

While she studied Ziggy, Francois announced Georges' absence. "Monsieur Loinger had business to attend to today, so I'm afraid you're stuck with me." He poked his mustache out in a silly pout. "How about a nice, friendly game of cat and mouse?"

The younger children whooped but Elka soured. Another one?

Ziggy must have sensed her rotten mood. "You don't like tag? Since when?"

She sighed, watching Peter run madly after Hettie. "It's odd Georges disappears so often, isn't it?"

She hadn't forgotten what Ziggy said that first day in the dining hall. About Georges being a spy.

"I guess he's busy," he said, punching her lightly on the shoulder.

"Hey! What was that for?"

"You're it!"

With that, Ziggy took off. Elka chased after him, grinning so hard her cheeks hurt.

An hour later, thunder clapped. Fat, freezing raindrops pierced the ground. The kids trudged inside and, over her shoulder, Elka glimpsed the tall firs and oaks at the edge of the forest. The canopy of trees was so thick, she thought it must provide nice cover from the rain. She imagined running the shady trails, listening to the rain shower's soft pitter-patter, a layer of soaked leaves cushioning her feet. The vision made her heart pound.

Tag hadn't been bad, but where in the world was Georges? No matter how hard they tried, Felix was never "it." No one could catch him, not even Elka. The Sports Festival wasn't exactly the Olympics, but it was a real competition. As much as she liked Felix, she wanted to be champion. Quickly, she shoved aside thoughts of shiny blue ribbons. A familiar sticky knot formed in her throat. Her days of running were behind her now.

Ziggy and Elka entered the hallway together. "What's that smell?" he asked her.

A piney scent greeted them. Elka stamped her wet shoes.

"Christmas trees," she said flatly. "They must be putting the decorations up."

Every year, the staff here went all out for Christmas. Huge wreaths adorned the doors, and Darcy tied big red bows on the banisters. There was a towering fir tree in the foyer, covered with strings of popcorn and foil ornaments and topped with an angel. Nestled beneath the tree were heaps of boxes wrapped in red and green. Her first year there, Elka learned they were stuffed with nothing but old newspapers to give them weight.

When she was little, Mama took her to downtown Berlin on winter holiday. They admired the twinkling lights dangling all over the city. They stuck their tongues out to catch snowflakes as they walked, gaping at candy cane stripes and twines of garland circling the streetlamps. Elka had felt tipsy from the color and sparkle of it all. Her family didn't celebrate Christmas, but she loved its glittery spectacle.

This charade, though, was a different story.

"What's wrong?" Ziggy asked when they reached the hearth room. He flopped into an armchair by the fireplace and stared at her.

"What do you mean?" She sank into the chair next to him, frowning at the red felt stockings hanging from the mantle.

Ziggy laughed. "*That's* what I mean. You don't like all the Christmas stuff?"

"I don't mind it." Elka pulled her knees to her chin. "It's just…"

She hesitated. She wasn't sure how to say what bothered her.

"We have a Christmas party every year. On Christmas Eve. Last year, Darcy even managed to get a goose."

"Ooh." Ziggy patted his stomach. "I can't remember the last time I ate goose."

"Yes, but…" Elka stared at the dancing flames. "Don't you think it's weird? Celebrating a holiday, you don't…celebrate?"

Ziggy paused. "Well, you're not really celebrating it. It's, you know, keeping up appearances. Just in case."

Just in case. Elka shivered and hugged her knees tighter. In case hateful men in brown came banging at the door again.

"I know. I like the tinsel and toy soldier Nutcrackers, I just…never mind." She extended her legs; fire warmed the soles of her feet. "I hope Georges is back tomorrow. Playing tag was alright, but it's not the same as run—I mean, as calisthenics."

Ziggy laughed. "C'mon on, Elka. You're not fooling anyone."

"What do you mean?"

"You're obsessed with the Sports Festival…with racing. Why don't you admit it?"

Her heart did a funny flip. "I'm not obsessed."

"You are, Elk. It's okay. You love running, I saw it in your face during the relay. The day Georges told us about the festival. So why pretend it's not a big deal?"

"Because…" she swallowed. "Because other than gym, the last time I really ran was the night… you know."

Then she couldn't stop the flow of memories. *Kristallnacht.* She knew Ziggy wanted to forget that torturous evening he'd spent hiding in fear with his mother.

She closed her eyes. "Mama made dumplings for dinner. She made the best dumplings."

Her family had sat down to eat when someone knocked on the door. Knock wasn't the right word for it. *Pounding.* Pounding so loud and hard, the crystal goblets on the table rattled.

"Open up!" a voice growled.

Mama froze. A rushing sound filled Elka's ears, and everything moved slower, like the kitchen was under water. Papa stood and walked to the door.

Then Nazis stormed inside. One pushed the tip of his bayonet into Papa's back and shoved him—like he was a criminal, not a tailor having dinner with his family.

"Everyone outside!" another yelled, pointing a rifle.

At Mama. At Ruth. At Elka.

That thawed Mama, who grabbed her arm and pulled her close.

Elka's insides turned to putty. She grabbed Ruth's hand and squeezed it. The three of them stumbled out of their home, onto the street. Shards of glass crackled under her sister's Mary Jane shoes.

On both sides of the lane, she saw the same horror playing out. In neighbors' front yards, women shrieked, and children wailed. She spotted Leah, a girl two years older than her. Their eyes met, Elka locked on Leah's terrified face.

She saw Leah's father yank his arms free from a storm trooper's grip. He ran towards Leah and her mother. Then Elka saw the brownshirt lift his bayonet…

"Do as they say," she heard Papa cry out. Two policemen forced him into the back of a car, he pressed his face against the foggy window. Elka tried to yell, but no sound came out.

Then Mama kneeled in front of her, with eyes wide and pleading. "Elka, take your sister and run as fast as you can."

"No!" Ruth clung to Mama's waist and buried her face. Mama choked back tears and stroked Ruth's hair.

"You must go with Elka, *schatzi*," she cooed. "She wants to give you a piggy-back ride."

Elka wanted to bawl. She wanted to cling to Mama's bodice, too. She wanted to feel Mama's hand smoothing her hair. But seeing her shell-shocked little sister gave her the courage of a lioness.

"Come on, Ruth! Let's go for a piggy-back ride!"

Mama forced a smile. It was a smile Elka would see in her dreams over and over for the next four years. A dream that would turn into a nightmare.

Sometimes, she imagined how it should have gone. Ruth climbing onto her back. Elka pressing her sister's legs to her sides. Mama embracing both girls, kissing them goodbye. Then Elka would *run*.

Why had she trained all those months if she was helpless now? All the hills she'd run up and down, building her strength, her endurance. What was the point if she couldn't save Ruth? She saw it plainly, how she'd outrun the men and their dreadful pistols. How she'd tear through the glass-strewn streets with her little sister on her back, not stopping until they were safe.

But that's not how it went.

"Please!" she begged. She reached for her sister. Ruth clung to Mama tighter and sobbed. Behind them, Elka saw one of the Nazis raise a torch.

The smell stung her nostrils. One moment, she was standing in front of Mama and Ruth. The next, she was running—to get as far away from the heat and screams as she could.

But she was also running away from Mama. And from Ruth.

Elka ran for what seemed like hours. Every time she turned a corner, she saw the same awful scene. She didn't stop, didn't slow her blistering pace.

"I left her behind. She was supposed to come with me. That's what Mama wanted. I was supposed to give her a piggy-back ride. But I left her. I left *them*."

She flinched, reliving the painful night out loud. Many times, she'd told herself she'd done what she could, but it was no use. She should've dragged Ruth kicking and screaming if that's what it took.

That was four years ago, when she was eight. She ran so far, she got lost, until a kind stranger urged her to join a group of kids escaping by train to France. Still, she should've done anything except run away—alone—saving only herself.

The guilt engulfed her like a tidal wave, rising higher and higher. It threatened to swallow her entire body. This was why it was best not to dwell on the past. She couldn't change it. No matter how much she wanted to.

"None of it matters," Elka said. "It happened, and that's that."

Ziggy seemed to collect his thoughts; the hearth fire crackled. There was little to say—nothing would make her pain go away. "But you shouldn't let that stop you from running now. You want to race, right? You want to win?"

Elka opened her mouth, wanting to say no. But then images from her old dreams flashed through her mind: putting on a surge of speed, passing her opponents, crossing the finish line, the roaring crowd…

"Yeah. I do."

"Well then, it's done. You need to start training. And I'm going to help you."

That night, Elka lay beneath her blankets, picturing snarky Jeannine whispering with Romilly. She waited until all the shuffling and shifting and shushing died down, then crept out of bed. She pulled open her sock drawer and reached for the neatly folded cloth in the back. Elka let her fingers graze the fabric but didn't lay it flat. She didn't want to look at it, and aside from sparks of gold thread, it was too dark to see, anyway.

Her father had been a great tailor. This was his last project; a prayer shawl—called a tallis—that a man in another city had commissioned him to sew. Papa had nearly been finished with it before the banging at their door—the moment that would change their lives forever. Each detail was engraved on her brain: Ruth's shiny Mary Janes, Papa's face against the glass, Mama pleading with Ruth to go with Elka. The frantic shouting, running as fast as she could, unaware she still held the tallis in her hands…

She gave her head a shake. Quickly, she closed her sock drawer. It was no use trying to sleep now, not with her pulse racing like crazy.

She walked over to the window. The woods behind the chateau boasted twisted oak trees. Giant pines also stretched upward, set against the starry sky, like something out of a fairy tale. Not all the ones she'd read had happy endings.

The children weren't allowed to go into the woods unsupervised, but Monsieur Francois led them on a nature walk once. Elka couldn't help noticing the trails were made of moist, soft bark.

Perfect for running.

She felt safe at the chateau, protected. She wasn't about to let hateful Jeannine Tremblay steal that feeling. Monsieur Francois and the rest of the staff wouldn't let anything bad happen to her, or to any of the others.

She had to cling to that hope. After all, hope was all she had left.

5

Ziggy

Ziggy had been dazzled by Elka, the day the Sports Festival was revealed—the way she ran with her ponytail floating behind her, her eyes glowing lanterns. Two winters had passed since he'd seen pure joy on someone's face. He wanted to hold on to that.

In June 1940, two years earlier, fighter planes thundered over Maison du Mouton— the orphanage in Versailles where Ziggy had lived before, not far from the famous palace of French kings. Threatened by aerial bomb attacks, France surrendered to the Germans.

Instead of the French flag, a black, crooked-cross swastika fluttered from ornate gates in the royal city.

After the German invasion, the children's long days in hiding were swept away by a darker, swifter undercurrent. Men in black helmets marched by Maison du Muton's rose gardens, and the number of Frenchmen in military uniforms multiplied, too. Were they forced into service, Ziggy wondered—or were they two-faced soldiers?

"Did you hear we're being assigned new last names that sound French instead of German?" Felix asked Ziggy, a month after the attack. He slid a saltshaker on the chess board two squares over. "That way, the authorities won't discover who we are. I'm told mine will be *Chambon*. I do love ham, you know?"

Ziggy blinked at the saltshaker, unamused. "Really?" His fingers hovered over a pine cone. The pine trees outside shed them like crazy in the fall, and he and Felix had collected them and painted some white and black, for castles; buttons they'd found in a chest of drawers became pawns. "Why do we need different names? The air raids are getting worse, but they haven't bothered with us."

Felix raised an eyebrow, but then his face softened. "No, I suppose not."

Back when Ziggy's father was fired, he'd insisted (at first) that things would be fine. Grownups did a lot more pretending than kids did.

"Your eyes look sad," he had told his father one morning at breakfast. He spread a swirling tornado of blackberry jam on his sourdough bread. "Can I cheer you up somehow?"

"The news is bad, son," his pa confessed. "It's not just the university shunning people like us. Even Tiergarten Park is closed to Jews now."

"Can we have our own classes?" Ziggy took a bite of toast. "How about we hold them right here, soon as I get home today. My teachers at the new school aren't so good anyway. You can tell me more about the German submarine that sank the British ship."

Pa smiled. "Ah, you mean the Lusitania. Almost 2,000 people lost their lives when she sank." He reached over, ruffled Ziggy's hair. "You're a perceptive boy. I'll prepare our lecture. Off you go to school, then—and don't forget your lunch."

That morning seemed like forever ago. Now Ziggy eyed Felix, who tapped a finger on the chess board. His Pa would've called Felix perceptive, too. He could see the core of people, like a radiograph.

"Don't worry," Felix said quietly. "Your name won't actually change. It's just because, well…I heard the nuns talking yesterday. The ones that taught us liturgy. They said the French police have orders to find Jewish kids, send us east. To the camps in Germany and Poland, where prisoners are beaten and starved. Our fake names are for the false papers the Jewish Scouts are forging for us. We need them in case…in case we have to leave. The Nazis haven't taken over in southern France."

"Yet," Ziggy whispered, under his breath. He knew some Jewish kids had fled half a dozen times, to stay a step ahead of the Nazi soldiers. But thinking about his father had made him feel brave. Even if it was fleeting. Even if Felix's warning scared him. "I can go by another name if it means they won't find us," Ziggy assured his friend.

"How is *Pommes*, then? Ziggy Pommes—potatoes have eyes, you know," Felix laughed. "And you're always watching for trouble."

"*C'est magnifique*," he forced a smile. "We eat so many I might turn into one!"

The truth was that nothing could save them from a Nazi raid. They would need to move to a whole new place…again.

Here in Annemasse, Ziggy still suspected Georges might betray them. The stronger Elka became, the better chance she had to outrun their enemies.

None of the adults could know he was conjuring a plan to help her run. They'd insist his idea was too dangerous. They'd warn she might encounter an officer in the woods. Ziggy already knew the risks. He and Elka would need to be very careful.

He set the plot in motion before sunrise the next morning.

"*Psst!* Elka!"

He stood outside the girls' dormitory. In the darkness, he saw the outline of Elka's long hair splayed over her pillow. In the bed opposite hers, Hettie stirred in her sleep.

Hopping on one foot, he took off his slipper. He inched closer to the open doorway—he didn't dare step inside, what if Francois caught him? —and took aim, tossing it high in the air.

The slipper landed right on Elka's stomach with a soft *plop*. She sat up and squinted at the crack of light coming from the hall. Ziggy put a finger to his lips.

She slipped out of bed, cinched her robe and rubbed her eyes. "Ziggy? What's going on—is something wrong?"

"Everything's fine. Runners rise early—you better get dressed."

Elka looked puzzled. "What do you mean?"

"I mean if you hurry, you can run three whole kilometers before breakfast. You know the trails in the woods behind us? If you take the side path by the veranda, there's only one window anyone could see you. The one in the study. I'll read a book there to block the view."

He fanned the novel Mademoiselle Bellegard gave him the day before. Elka gaped at him like a hooked fish.

"I can't let you do that! What if you get in trouble?"

"Never mind me. My father always said it's good to offer help, but better to accept it."

Her green eyes twinkled. "I'll do it."

"Then why are you still here? Get dressed." Ziggy massaged his left foot. "Meet me in the parlor. And don't forget my slipper."

At daybreak, while Ziggy sat by the drawing room window, Elka snuck out the door. The only time he put his book down was to stoke the hearth. As warmth crept across his skin, he was struck by a memory of Pa, seated in his favorite wingback chair. He would get so lost in reading he wouldn't notice how dark it was getting outside until Ma turned the lamp on.

She was always caring for his father that way. Six Hanukkahs ago, she gave Pa a new shaving kit. Inside its tan leather case were two soft-bristle brushes, cedar-scented cologne, and a double-edged razor. *Danka*, his father had said, kissing his mother on her forehead. Ziggy admired the razor's polished amber handle. When he was grown up enough, he'd lather his beard and shave like he'd seen his father do before work every day.

When it was Ziggy's turn to open a gift, he eagerly opened the blue foil box, sent by his aunt. Beneath layers of crisp white tissue, he found a book embossed in gold block letters: *Les Histoires de Patachou*. His aunt's bookstore, on its chic Paris street corner, stayed open past midnight on weekends. More than once, Ziggy had fallen asleep on its plush velvet chairs with mink throw pillows.

Having spent an entire month in the hospital with polio, reading was Ziggy's favorite pastime. Besides, he'd always been studious—his first school report described him as diligent. Occasionally, he attended his father's lectures (to give his mother a break from his endless streams of questions). Though he didn't fully understand the class discussions, Ziggy could feel his brain expanding on the spot.

With the glorious new Hanukkah book in his lap, he forgot about the rest of his presents—a wooden toy plane, a die-cast car. He knew books like this one cost a lot of money. When his mother called him for dessert—custard-filled fried donuts—he saved his place with a candy wrapper.

After dessert, his ma swayed to the music on the radio while the dishes soaked. Menorah candles lit up her face; her cotton evening dress twirled, tossing shadows on the wool rug. His father joined her, and the two of them danced like they were in a fancy ballroom.

Like the world was carefree, like they could stay on the dizzying carousel of this moment and never get off. Like the staticky music would play forever.

The candles flickered, dripping wax on the tablecloth. Ziggy's eyelids grew heavy. His father carried him to bed and gently pulled a patchwork quilt under his chin.

Soon, he drifted to sleep, dreaming of a walk alone in the woods. He wasn't sure where he was, but it was someplace far, far from home.

Suddenly, a twig snapped outside, jolting Ziggy from his daydream. He skimmed page nine of his novel, wondering *Would Pa like this story?* It was the sort of mystery his dad would finish in one sitting, skipping pages to search for clues.

Three chapters later, a breeze blew in, with Elka close behind. Her face was glossy and flushed. "Wait right here," Ziggy said, and went to check the hallway. Once he confirmed the coast was clear, she skipped upstairs to shower and change.

At breakfast, she spoke excitedly about her run. When she wasn't looking, Ziggy spooned his porridge into her bowl. If he tried to offer it, she'd refuse. Georges said athletes burned more energy, and though he didn't know altogether what to make of him, Ziggy believed that much.

The buzzy feeling of a shared secret stayed with him all day. In gym, he and Elka practiced passing on a diagonal—they rolled a leather ball back-and-forth, at least a hundred times. During shooting drills, Ziggy's ball catapulted over the wooden goalpost. But every one of Elka's shots went sailing to the back of the net.

At lunch, Ziggy poured his milk into Elka's empty cup, as she turned to talk to Hettie. The walk to school afterward was the only time he saw his friend without a smile. Jeannine threw a small rock at her, and missed, but barely—when the rock grazed Elka's arm, she winced.

For a moment, he was afraid Elka would get into a fight with Jeannine. Or worse, rat on Jeannine to Mademoiselle Bellegard. He disliked Jeannine, but he didn't want to rile a girl whose father held power in Annemasse.

But other than brushing imaginary dirt off her arm, Elka pretended she didn't notice. "Guess I'm not the only one who needs coaching," she joked to Ziggy, and the two of them laughed.

They swiftly fell into a new schedule. Every morning, Ziggy met Elka in the study before dawn, book in hand. She stole away to run a few kilometers while he kept watch. Sometimes he left his post to skim the newspaper, delivered to the front step, before Darcy had a chance to bring it inside. Before it was used for fireplace kindling.

MORE JEWS CAPTURED IN VICHY RAIDS, the headline read.

Then Elka would return in just enough time to bathe and eat breakfast. In the evenings, once the pair finished after-supper chores, they'd repeat the routine.

If Monsieur Francois learned Elka was running in the woods with Ziggy's help, they'd be scolded. Georges would forbid it too if he knew. But would his concern be fake, like stagecraft?

One morning before class, Ziggy swayed Elka into snooping on Georges. "Did you notice he disappears after breakfast? Where does he go?"

She sighed. "It's none of our business. Not everything Georges does is our business."

"Or maybe it is," Ziggy argued. "We'll never know unless we try to find out."

Finally, she agreed they'd trail their teacher—together. "Like a pair of undercover detectives," she laughed.

"It's not funny," he said, scowling. "There he goes, c'mon!"

He tugged her arm, and the two of them tiptoed behind their teacher. Georges walked briskly, so although Elka had initially resisted their plan, she nudged Ziggy to keep up. He knew every corner of the chateau—he'd explored it many times, looking for secret passageways, like the one he and Felix had discovered at Maison du Muton. In case they'd need escape routes at a minute's notice.

Soon Georges entered a storage room. Ziggy and Elka squeezed behind the open door and held their breath. "Shirts and sneakers are costly. Not to mention, difficult to find. The kids need new ones for the festival," they heard him say.

Why wouldn't Georges ask the OSE for children's clothes? If that's who he really worked for?

"I'll see what I can do. No promises," a man answered, followed by a coughing fit. Ziggy recognized the voice. Mayor Deffaugt!

Ziggy and Elka exchanged troubled looks. Later, at lunch, the two of them huddled together, reviewing what they'd overheard. "See what I mean Elka? Why would Georges meet with the mayor—in a storage closet of all places. I told you there's something strange going on."

She threw up her hands. "They were talking about how we need more clothes to wear. What's the big deal? We're safe here."

We're all being fooled! Ziggy wanted to shout. Getting Elka to see that would be harder than he thought. But she would keep training for the sports day. Ziggy would make sure of that. She wore layers for warmth; her gray wool sweater was perfect for camouflage. If soldiers were on patrol at dawn, she'd be difficult to see.

In fact, Ziggy guessed the woods were safer than the chateau. A few weeks ago, he'd listened to the British radio broadcast. The leader of the French Resistance, Charles de Gaulle, delivered frightening news: the Nazis were gaining hold in France. They now occupied Vichy, a short three-hour train ride from Annemasse.

A few of the children, like Hettie, were shocked. He couldn't understand why. They knew southern France was declared a "free zone" under the rule of Marshal Philippe Pétain. But Pétain was in league with Hitler! This part of the country was really no freer than Paris, where swastikas draped from the Arc de Triomphe during Nazi soldiers' military parades.

The reality of German troops closing in was terrifying, no question. But wasn't it worse *not* to know things? Wasn't it better to be ready for what was coming next?

Ziggy hadn't prepared for the news almost six years ago, when soldiers arrested his father. He hadn't prepared to hide in old Frau Wagner's attic for half a year, sleeping on a musty mattress, where moths chewed holes in his single thin blanket, so his toes grew numb when the weather was cold. And any noise—the cat knocking over a houseplant downstairs, a woodpecker's racket—sent him shivering with fear.

He hadn't prepared to watch Ma grow thinner and thinner, insisting Ziggy eat the lion's share of whatever Frau Wagner left them at the top of the ladder that night. A bowl of scorched oatmeal, moldy brie.

Ever since he left Berlin, he made a silent vow never to be off-guard again.

On the last day of school before Christmas, Ziggy struggled to concentrate on the book Mademoiselle gave him that morning. Elka practiced grammar on the blackboard. As usual, they'd arrived early before their teacher tugged the bell pull. He'd been unable to sleep the night before. His tired eyes watered, making it impossible to read.

The tap of Elka's scrawl began lulling him to sleep, when muffled sobs came from the hallway. Waking from his catnap, Ziggy's head snapped up. The door was open wide enough to catch a glimpse of Mademoiselle Bellegard, her arm around Hettie's quivering shoulders. Hettie held a piece of paper by her side.

While Elka riddled out a French conjugation, he stood up and limped from the classroom. He quietly closed the door and peered down the hallway. There was Hettie, leaving with her head cast downward.

"What's wrong?" he asked his teacher. "Is she okay?"

Mademoiselle's eyes were moist. "She's alright," she said and placed a reassuring hand on his arm. "A letter was delivered for her at school today. It was from her mother."

Ziggy's head throbbed. He tried to imagine what it must be like, knowing your mother was still alive. To see her handwriting, to read words she'd written just for you.

"Ziggy," Mademoiselle Bellegard said softly. "Are *you* okay?"

He straightened. "I'm fine."

"Are you sure?"

He nodded. "Can you ask Hettie not to tell Elka about that letter?"

His teacher raised an eyebrow. "Why?"

Her question stumped him. How could he explain? "Because…because she thinks her family is still alive. If she finds out Hettie heard from her mother, she'll start hoping to hear from her parents. Or from her—her little sister."

Like a sputtering engine, he choked on the words. Then Mademoiselle Bellegard spoke, her voice barely above a whisper.

"And why do you think hope is a bad thing?"

"I don't think it's *bad*. It's…unrealistic." He wanted to tell Mademoiselle about the last time Elka saw her family. The suffocating flames, the panic and shouting. He wanted to share every awful detail so his teacher would understand what he knew: she might never see her sister or her parents again.

Mademoiselle Bellegard sighed. "It might be unrealistic. But hope and faith are powerful feelings, Ziggy. Especially in times like this." She paused. "Try not to let go of yours. Okay?"

Have faith. Ziggy could see those two words in his father's neat penmanship.

Pa had faith. Look where it got him.

But Mademoiselle was watching him with her kind, gray eyes. Ziggy couldn't bring himself to tell her the truth: he let go of hope and faith a long time ago.

6

Elka

Every bitter-cold February morning, Elka rose a few minutes earlier. And every evening, she crawled into bed a tiny bit later. Even though the time she slept shrank, night by night, and her ribs showed like ripples under her skin, Elka was bursting with energy. It was electric—a constant tingling up and down her arms and legs.

Training consumed her waking hours. With the wood trail ahead, she ran free. She'd mark distances mentally—a tree stump, a stream. Three kilometers every morning turned to four, then five as she focused on going farther and faster. Nights were for sprinting and speed work; a hilly clearing a half kilometer away allowed her to run all out, without worrying about tripping over a root in the dark.

But there was another reason she craved running. A private reason. One she hadn't confided in Ziggy.

The first time it happened was a frigid morning two weeks before. She shivered as she ran, the cold nipping her slight arms through the frayed sleeves of her sweater. Silver light outlined the slate snow clouds overhead, a signal to turn back soon—she couldn't risk getting caught sneaking in, or Ziggy might also get into trouble. But the second kilometer mark was in front of her, which meant it would be two more back. If she pushed herself, she could finish in under fifteen minutes.

There! Elka saw the splintered 2, carved on a tree up ahead. Ziggy once spent an entire afternoon tagging her route. She circled the tree and headed back up the path.

Four kilometers! Almost there.

The muscles in her legs burned. Her lungs seared with each breath of biting wind. But she pushed herself harder. How high was the sun? She couldn't tell because a thick blanket of clouds covered it. She pictured Ziggy waiting anxiously, then Monsieur Francois discovering him right as she burst through the door, windburned and perspiring…

Faster. Elka ignored the pain in her legs. She exploded with speed.

Six kilometers. Seven. Eight…

That was when she thought she saw a shadow the size of a small child.

It was so unexpected, so out of place, she stumbled on a root. The shadow was impossibly fast, so even when Elka regained her balance she couldn't catch it. It was airy and nimble and slipped through the trees at high speed, then vanished from sight.

She rubbed her eyes and flew down the path. She reached the last kilometer and blasted through the trees, into the turnip garden. Slowing to a trot, she gasped for air. She spun a full circle but saw no one.

Who else would be out here running this early? Greta? No, Greta was sound asleep in her bed when she snuck out—all the girls were. Besides, Greta couldn't run faster than her.

No one could, except Felix. And that hadn't been Felix's shadow.

Elka sank to the frozen ground, and put her head between her legs, panting. Maybe her mind was playing tricks on her but nothing would stop her from running.

<hr />

By mid-March, the earth thawed and teardrop-shaped buds formed on the trees. Elka's morning runs lasted longer, even as her body grew frailer. She often left the chateau before Ziggy was awake, but always returned to find him at the drawing room window.

She didn't tell him about the shadow. That she was seeing things. She didn't tell anyone. While her lace-up boots beat a rhythm on the path, the shadow skipped over bushes, through branches.

Like a ghost.

This, if she was being honest, was the real reason she never told Ziggy. Because he was a wary boy, and if she tried telling him there was a ghost running in the woods with her, he'd insist she'd been training too hard. Or worse, gone mad.

And maybe she had. She climbed into bed after midnight, her calves screaming from hours of hill sprints. She woke less than four hours later and squeezed her blistered feet back into her shoes. This wasn't just about winning the race anymore.

Right now, chasing the shadow, it didn't matter. Again and again, she saw its silhouette, and then the swift figure darted from view.

The first warm spring morning, Elka got up at four and crept outside. Her heart pounded with anticipation, drowning out the sound of her growling stomach. She touched her toes, then took off down the moonlit trail.

She picked up speed. Her grainy eyes scanned spruce trees, but no sign of the shadow. *It's all in your head,* she told herself. She was so intent on spotting it she didn't hear the voices until it was almost too late.

She came to a halt, her heart hammering for another reason besides her run. There were men in the woods. At least two of them. And they were steps behind her.

The first few weeks Elka trained, she'd worried Nazi soldiers would trip her up. But after months without seeing anyone—except for the shadow—she forgot her worst fears. Was she reckless to think the forest was safe for a Jewish girl running alone?

She veered off the path and crouched under an oak. Its broad, papery leaves cloaked her gaunt figure. She clamped a hand to her mouth and listened as the men drew closer.

Dry bark cracked. "…sure it will work?"

She recognized that voice. The men stopped a tree stump away.

"It's a risk, but a calculated one. I believe it will work."

"They're frightened."

"I know they're frightened. But this may be their only chance."

Slowly, cautiously, Elka peeked around the trunk. There, on the trail up ahead, was Georges.

His face sagged with fatigue. Right then, it struck her that his rosy outlook took work. To Ziggy, it was deceitful, but she wasn't as mistrusting. Whenever she played soccer in gym class, she felt like a regular kid again.

She told Ziggy he read too many detective stories. But wait—what was Georges doing so deep in the forest?

"You're right. We must go through with it—before it's too late," the stranger said. Elka squinted—he looked barely older than Felix. His coal black hair framed high cheekbones. "Tomorrow at two, then?"

"Tomorrow at two."

Georges shook the young man's hand, then pulled him into a swift hug. The man turned to hike farther into the woods, and Georges started in Elka's direction.

She ducked behind the tree trunk. Adrenaline coursed through her body. Getting caught in the woods by her gym teacher would be way less disastrous than being seized by soldiers—wouldn't it? —but she would prefer not to get caught at all.

She and Ziggy had snooped on Georges' meeting in the supply room with Mayor Deffaugt. Plus, Georges missed the occasional gym class, always returning the next day without explanation. Now he was holding secret meetings in the woods before dawn. What had this been about?

I know they're frightened. But this may be their only chance.

She bristled. What was Georges discussing? Did it have anything to do with her and the other children? Who was the other strange man?

She was desperate to tell Ziggy about her surprise encounter. Something about it made her trust Georges even more. But at this early hour, Ziggy would still be in bed. Lately, he'd insisted she needed more rest, too. But with the Sports Festival a month away, Elka couldn't spare a day of training. She waited until the trees completely obscured Georges, then edged back onto the trail.

As she ran, she replayed the conversation she'd overheard. She had to tell Ziggy he'd been right about one thing: Georges wasn't just their gym teacher.

This might be urgent. Instead of running another meter, Elka turned back.

When she reached the chateau, she saw Ziggy's profile through the study window. He was awake after all, waiting for her. She double-checked that no one was watering the garden, then zipped down the path and into the drawing room.

The door closed behind her, Ziggy looked up. "The moon's still out, Elk. You promised to sleep in today."

"He *is* a spy."

"What?"

"Georges. A spy. I saw him."

Elka plunked into the chair opposite Ziggy and told him everything she'd seen and heard. As she spoke, his eyes widened.

"Do you think the other man was a Nazi?" he asked.

Elka shook her head. "I don't think so, no. He wasn't wearing a uniform."

"That doesn't mean he's not a German soldier."

"They were speaking French."

"So? We speak French, and we're German." Ziggy drummed his fingers, eyes adrift. Like he was studying something she couldn't see.

"So...is he? Doesn't this prove he's a spy?" she finally said.

"He's a sneak, that's for sure. And well, there's the Sports Festival."

"What about it?"

He yawned nervously and rubbed his knee. "We're already exhausted from doing schoolwork and washing dishes and mopping floors. Then all his training zaps us too. Darcy tries her best, but we hardly have enough to eat. Why would this be the right time to have a festival 'for fun'?"

"Because..." Elka's voice trailed off. He had a point. She'd been so excited about the sports day, so looking forward to it, she hadn't questioned why they were having one.

Then it dawned on her again—the smile Georges wore disguised his worries. "To give us a reason to be happy. Most of the girls cry themselves to sleep every night, and I bet it's the same for the boys, right? Georges wants to do something nice for us."

"That's what I try telling myself," Ziggy said. "But I don't know. If he's meeting a stranger undercover in the woods in the middle of the night…what if he's up to something else?"

Elka quieted. Ziggy's father had been part of a secret group, protesting the Nazis. Then double-crossed by someone he'd thought was trustworthy. Yet Georges was so kind. With him teaching gym, her days were bearable. Besides, some spies were on their side, weren't they? The thought of a betrayal made her stomach queasy.

"You said they plan to meet again?" Ziggy asked.

"Tomorrow at two." Then Ziggy met her gaze, and she knew what he was thinking before he said it.

"Let's follow him."

The next morning, Elka took extra caution on her run. She walked the first kilometer—she was exhausted anyhow—and listened closely for voices. Nothing met her ears but the scuff of her shoes. When she knew she was alone, she picked up her feet and ran.

The shadow didn't appear until she reached the halfway point. She chased it all the way back to the chateau. When she got to the garden trellis, she clutched her side.

She'd been so close this time, close enough to reach out and touch its swinging braids.

But she knew those weren't really braids. They were tree branches. Maybe Ziggy was right, she needed rest. She thought of the shadow all day, moving through lessons like a zombie.

On the walk from school for lunch, Ziggy confronted her.

"Did you change your mind?"

"What?"

"Shhh." He scouted the street. "You know. About spying on Georges. We'll have to follow him right after gym."

Elka had been so preoccupied with the shadow she'd forgotten their detective mission. "No, I'm still in. Are you?"

"Yeah, I'm in."

Good, because you're wrong about Georges, she thought. No chance such a gentle man was up to anything wicked. But she knew her friend needed proof, and she hoped they'd get it.

That afternoon in gym, Felix filled in to coach, while Georges worked on free kicks with the little ones. Before class was up, the older kids scrimmaged.

"I'm open!" Ziggy shouted to Felix, who dribbled up-field and sent the ball his direction. Ziggy trapped it with his foot, then took a shot on goal. Hettie, who practiced passing with Sophia on the sideline, ran to the ball while Ziggy jogged backward…and stopped. He rubbed his hip while his teammates snaked around him.

"Ziggy, take a break," Felix called out.

The rest of the group resumed the game, with Elka at striker position. She mused Felix was more than a talented runner—his feet were quicker than wheels on a car. No one could steal the ball from him, but he could take it from anyone. He faked them all out with a skillful dance, then galloped downfield.

"Nice job," she wheezed when he scored again.

Felix hadn't broken a sweat. "Thanks," he shrugged. She watched him jog back to center and shook her head. One day, she thought, she'd see Felix playing in the World Cup.

If they all outlasted the war.

When class was over, the younger kids scrambled to scoop up loose balls. Georges strolled into the chateau, smiling to himself; Elka and Ziggy hid behind the shed and waited.

After a short while, Georges returned. He wore an ink-colored suit and fedora and whistled while he walked. "That's weird," Ziggy mumbled. "Why is he all dressed up?"

They let him walk for several blocks before lurking behind. Down Rue de la Gare, past brick-and-stone apartment buildings where purple petunias decorated balconies. They snuck behind hedges or parked cars for cover in case Georges looked back.

When he climbed the steps of a domed cathedral, Elka saw her excitement mirrored on Ziggy's face. She knew their quest was shaky—Francois would throw an absolute fit if he found out—but it was a thrill to be prowling around like this.

Instead of opening the church's front door, Georges sauntered around back, past its stained-glass windows. Elka and Ziggy pursued him to the entry of a public park. A water fountain spouted from a cherub-like figure, and a young couple passed, holding hands.

"Are you sure they didn't say where their meeting is?" Ziggy whispered.

"I'm positive. Maybe we should sneak back and wait for another chance to figure out what he's up to."

As soon as those words left her lips, Ziggy grabbed her arm. "Look!" he hissed and pulled her behind a shrub. She peered through the evergreen stems. When she saw Georges welcoming a handful of children, her heart gave an extra hard thump.

All of them were dressed in black, like him.

She recognized one in the group, right away. "That's the same man he met in the woods." she told Ziggy in a hushed tone. "But who are those kids?"

"I don't know." He stared as Georges embraced the young man. Both wore somber expressions. The children fidgeted.

They're frightened, Georges had said.

This didn't feel like a game anymore.

Georges led everyone, single file, through the parkway into an open plaza. They cut across it to the sidewalk, marching on for three more blocks. To their left stood a tall steel gate, with a sea of granite headstones scattered behind it.

Ziggy moaned. A cemetery? What could this mean? The group wove through the graveyard and disappeared among the tombstones.

Elka's shoulders sank. "A funeral. That must be it. Georges had a funeral to attend."

She knew Ziggy felt as awful as she did. As disappointed, too. Then out of nowhere, he tugged the back of her romper. Quickly, she squatted down.

"What are you—" she began. Then she heard voices, and the clunk of boots on cobblestones.

Soldiers.

Ziggy pointed to a white Volkswagen parked a few feet away. They crawled over, wiggling underneath—Ziggy lying between the two front tires, Elka squeezed between the back ones. She froze in place as the soldiers passed. When their footsteps faded, she exhaled. She wiped her clammy hands on her skirt and let them rest on her hips.

"That was close."

Ziggy didn't budge. "W-we should wait before heading back," he said.

"I know. Oh my gosh. Whoa, that was close." Elka stammered, straining to see around the tire. "But who were those kids with Georges? Has he mentioned having a family?"

"No—I mean, not that I remember."

They fell silent at the clump of gleaming boots. Another soldier marched past and Elka shuddered. What were they thinking, spying on poor, mourning Georges? Now they were stuck under a parked car, and guards roamed nearby.

Minutes dragged on before either spoke a word.

"Elka?" Ziggy finally said.

"What? More officers?"

"No. It's Georges."

She looked out from behind the tire. There was her gym teacher, departing the graveyard with the young man. It was strange, though. Instead of appearing sad, they slapped each other on the back. Elka's belly rocked like a leaky rowboat.

Georges and the man wandered away, down the street. Over the smattering of tombstones, she could see the woods on the other side. There wasn't a single child in sight.

"Where are those children?" Ziggy blurted. "Where did they go?"

Elka opened her mouth, but nothing came out.

What had Georges done?

7

Ziggy

Ziggy stared at the ceiling all night.

For one thing, his leg ached from hiding with Elka under the automobile earlier that day. Finally, they'd managed to get back to their feet and flee.

The image of those children in the cemetery haunted him. One minute they were there with Georges. The next they'd vanished. He tossed and turned, his bunk bed caw-cawing like a crow. At last, he fell asleep, thinking of a map of Annemasse he'd found in the study that afternoon. This one was detailed with place markers. There was one entrance to the graveyard, on its south side—no east or west exits, and the north side was bordered by a wall.

"It doesn't make sense," Ziggy said to Elka for the thousandth time at breakfast. "Why would Georges and his friend ditch the children in the graveyard like that? Was there ever a funeral at all?"

Elka scraped her spoon in the bowl. She'd emptied it in three bites. Maybe it was his imagination, but she looked like a paper doll, like the slightest breeze could blow her away. Her cheeks were drawn, her eyes were sunken and dull—not their usual, fir-tree green.

"How was your run this morning?" he asked, silently wishing she'd skipped it like she swore she would.

"Not bad." She licked the bowl clean. "Better now that it's warmer outside. No more frozen toes after the first kilometer."

No denying Elka was determined. She'd committed to training all winter. But were her runs making her sickly instead of stronger, now? If there were people with bad intentions among them, she mustn't weaken.

When she cocked her head back to take a drink, he spooned his leftovers in her bowl.

Let Elka focus on winning the race, he told himself. *I'll worry about Georges.*

Another chance to spy came two days later. After supper, Mademoiselle Bellegard surprised them with a stack of new books from the library. Ziggy plucked *Of Mice and Men* from her tilting pile before she could shelve it. He settled into his chair and opened to page one…when someone outside caught his eye.

He pressed his nose to the windowpane and tried to make out the figure. The purple dusk made it hard to see a face, but he could tell it was a man. A stout man wearing a familiar, drab uniform.

Ziggy dropped the book into his lap. Dread slithered up his spine like a snake.

The man marched by the window, past the front entrance. He wore his cap pulled low, and now that he was closer, Ziggy saw his right sleeve was stitched in red, white, and blue—French flag colors. French military decorations, not German ones, covered the front of his chest.

Not a Nazi soldier. Ziggy knew from reading the newspaper that many French militia didn't answer to the Vichy regime—despite Pétain's displeasure. The legion volunteers who did figured it was better than being sent to forced labor in Germany. They decided it was easier to fight for your enemy than against him. That logic didn't make much sense to Ziggy.

He set his novel on the end table as the man turned behind the chateau. Feet pattered upstairs. The younger children were preparing for bed. Ziggy got up and limped down the corridor.

Why wasn't this man using the front door? It all seemed deeply ominous.

Was he here to meet with Georges, too?

He reached the end of the hall and put an ear to the wall. Footsteps click-clacked from the south wing… someone was letting the stranger in.

"Ziggy?"

He spun around to see Elka standing there, her cheeks splotched, pink. "Elka!" he shout-whispered. "What are you—"

"I saw him coming down the street, so I came back," she panted. "That's Jeannine Tremblay's father."

Fear shot through Ziggy. Commander Tremblay, head of the local legion of French soldiers! He should have recognized him right away.

"Do you think he's here to see Georges?" she asked. The back door opened, followed by muffled conversation, and the two kids traded looks. Ziggy knew they were thinking the same thing. The Nazis occupied the Free

Zone in Vichy. If roundups were taking place there, would they happen here, next? Whoever Commander Tremblay had come to see, a legion boss's visit to a home hiding Jewish orphans couldn't be good.

Jeannine made her father's disgust for them perfectly clear months ago. He'd give them up like a pack of stray dogs if it meant gaining power.

The voices faded. Ziggy and Elka slunk toward the rear entrance. They saw the back of Commander Tremblay as he walked into the library. The pair crept farther down the hallway when they heard, "I'm so sorry to disturb you, but you have a visitor."

The two of them crouched down. That was Monsieur Francois's voice. Did he know Commander Tremblay was here to see Georges?

But when an answer came, it wasn't Georges speaking.

"It's no trouble," a cheery voice trilled. Mademoiselle Bellegard! "How did you know I would be here, Commander?"

"My daughter told me you often visit Francois's establishment with book donations," came the commander's smooth reply. "Very generous of you, Mademoiselle."

"The generosity is all the donors. We're grateful for their gifts. I'm simply bringing them by. Now, what can I do for you? Is this regarding Jeannine's schoolwork?"

"No, no, nothing like that. Are you aware of the rally in support of Marshal Pétain?"

"*Another* one?" Mademoiselle replied with an easy laugh, though her tone quickly cooled. "It seems they're becoming weekly events."

"It's important for the entire community to show support for our leader," Commander Tremblay went on, dismissing her comment. "*All* citizens…even the children. As local leader of the Legion of French Volunteers, and a proud father of one of these young citizens, I'm requesting your assistance. I would like your students to attend this Saturday. They should be ready to wave flags for Pétain as he passes."

A pause followed. Ziggy couldn't see him, but he imagined Commander Tremblay flexing his fingers like crawling spiders. Mademoiselle Bellegard would be wearing that expression she saved for misbehaving or disrespectful pupils—a straight-lipped look of exasperation.

"I'm happy to inform my students of the rally," Mademoiselle replied. "And I can certainly encourage them to make an appearance...with their families of course."

"You misunderstand me. This must be a required event. For *all* students."

"I see." Mademoiselle sighed. "Unfortunately, I'm afraid I can't guarantee their attendance. Only their parents can give such permission—it isn't up to their teacher."

There was a long, awkward silence. Ziggy's leg throbbed from squatting so long. He'd pay a price for this later.

"You're right." Commander Tremblay's voice hardened. "That is, those who have parents to provide that permission."

His last sentence crushed Ziggy like a boulder. He could almost feel the floorboards sink beneath his feet. The commander knew they weren't traumatized survivors of the Marseilles shelling, here to regain their health.

They were fleeing a government controlled by Nazi tyrants, skulking closer, bent on wiping them out.

"Quite true, Commander," Mademoiselle replied. "Many of the residents here haven't heard from their families in some time, especially those with fathers bravely fighting for our country. But rest assured, I will do my best to notify them about the rally."

Hearing this, Ziggy wanted to jump up and hug his teacher. She and Francois could be charged with treason for hiding Jews. Yet here she was, standing up to a legion boss.

"It's a dangerous game you're playing," Commander Tremblay spat. "Your cooperation is expected. I look forward to seeing you and your students on Saturday."

Elka's fingernails dug into Ziggy's arm. He realized—too late—the commander was exiting the library. They'd never make it down the corridor in time. Alarmed, he shot to his feet, ignoring the stabbing pain in his thigh. Elka rushed to the closet across the hall.

He started telling her *don't bother*—that closet was always locked because it held cleaning supplies like bleach—but she was already pulling a hairpin from her ponytail. After a couple seconds of wiggling, inside the lock, she pushed the door open and pulled Ziggy in with her.

The door latch clicked, the room was black. A strong ammonia smell made Ziggy dizzy. They waited silently until the sound of the commander's footsteps disappeared.

"He—he knows," Elka finally whispered. "Jeannine's father knows."

Ziggy couldn't take the chemical aroma a second longer. He opened the door a sliver, inhaled through his nose. Light from the hall illuminated Elka's scared face, and his heart cracked in half.

This is what hope gets you, Elka, he couldn't help thinking. *It's no use clinging to useless dreams that everything will be okay. Reality always catches up in the end.*

He looked away. On the shelf next to him, a small mirror caught his eye. He leaned closer, studied his reflection. There was a smudge above his lip, but when he tried to brush it off, it wouldn't budge. Facial hair.

A sudden, unbearable longing to hear his pa's voice, to see his proud smile, hit Ziggy. What would Pa say, if he were here? Not about the mustache, but about Commander Tremblay, the rally…and most importantly, Elka?

He could hear his father's words. As if he were standing here in the cramped closet with them. *Helping others is the one thing you'll never regret.*

He turned to face Elka. Her blouse hung like drapes from her bony shoulders. But worse—her face was haunted.

"You should go on your run," he suggested. "It's early enough."

She wiped her wet eyes. "I'm not sure I'm up to it."

"What will make you feel better? Lying in bed thinking about Jeannine's father? Or running?"

Her bottom lip twitched. "Running."

He pushed the door open and smiled. "I'll be on the lookout in the study."

"Okay. Thanks, Zig," she said, before heading down the hall. He watched her do side bends while she walked. She would get stronger again. He would make sure of it, even if it meant he had to give up his breakfast every morning.

He would never tell her this in a thousand years, but his motivation wasn't really the Sports Festival. Ziggy knew, after Commander Tremblay's visit, what was ahead. Sooner or later, they would both end up deported to Germany or Poland. But if Elka was strong, if she was healthy, she would have a chance to survive.

Unlike him. He would have no chance at all.

8

Elka

Elka ran faster than she had in her whole life.

No hill tonight. She stuck to the overgrown trail, her eyes adjusting to the darkness. Commander Tremblay's words clattered in her skull like pebbles. *Those who have parents.*

A lump rose in her throat, she gulped it down. *Faster*, she thought, and her body obeyed, as if she could outrun his cruel words. *Faster. Fast—*

A shadow sped by her. "Come back here!" she begged. But it taunted her with a shimmery wave, then sprinted down the path.

The shock sparked Elka on. She ran all-out, eyes glued to the shadow. It had never taken such a clear shape. She saw its fair skin and flowing pigtails, as if it wasn't a shadow at all—but a girl. A young girl with shiny hair tied in pink ribbons to match her rose-colored dress, her patent leather shoes sparkling in the dark...

Recognition flooded Elka. A cry escaped her lips.

The shadow flitted, in and out of the mist and the trees like a delicate bird. She didn't think twice—she plowed through the brush, ignoring the thorns cutting her arms and legs, looking around frantically for any sign of movement.

"*Ruth!*"

Her own shout brought Elka to her senses. There was no sign of anyone, no sound other than her own shrill voice.

That night, she dreamed the forest was on fire.

It started with a maple tree. She was running her normal route, her first stretch to the one-kilometer mark. At first, she thought its leaves were turning color, like it was autumn again. Then she saw the roaring flames.

They spread with dangerous speed, igniting the trail, creating an inferno that mushroomed into a white-hot ceiling. Elka skidded to a stop. Then she heard her sister's cry.

"Elka! *Help!*"

Her mind blanked. She ran into the flames. Fire licked her arms and legs as she searched for Ruth. This time, *this* time, she vowed not to let her little sister cling to Mama. She would lift Ruth onto her back, and together, they would flee.

But she couldn't see her sister. The scorching blaze closed in, burning hotter and higher. Elka heard Ruth's loud whimpers, but she couldn't tell where they were coming from. She whirled and whirled until at last, a scream ripped loose from her throat—

"Elka!"

Gasping for air, she bolted upright in bed. Then Hettie sat up, eyes puffy and alarmed. Soon the other girls in the dormitory were awake too. They all stared at her.

"Sorry. Bad dream."

One by one, the girls lay back down. Hettie remained propped against her pillow, hair mussed like it was windblown. "That must've been a dreadful nightmare," she said in a trembling voice.

Elka felt terrible for scaring her. "Just a dream," she reassured her friend. The girl smiled weakly and leaned back on her pillow. After a few minutes, Elka heard her soft snores.

But she lay awake for hours afterward, curled on her side, gazing out the window. She couldn't tell anyone, not even Ziggy—they'd all think she'd gone mad, and she couldn't blame them. She couldn't shake Ruth's memory—and what she'd failed to do for her sister four years ago.

Save her.

Sunlight warmed Elka's face. The inside of her eyelids glowed orange. She sat up and glanced around. She was so used to rising in blackness, the brightness of the dormitory felt wrong, threatening. The bunks were abandoned, covers taut, neatly made.

She flung herself out of bed. Not only had she slept through her morning run, but she'd also slept *late*. Had she missed gym? Georges said there'd be soccer conditioning, one-on-one attacking drills. Why hadn't

Hettie, or any of the girls, woken her? Why hadn't Ziggy?

What was going on?

She pulled on a skirt, ran downstairs, and flew out the door to Avenue Florissant. The clear blue sky and cheerful bird chirps grated her nerves. Elka blinked, chasing away the shadow image in her mind. She couldn't explain how she knew it, but something was wrong.

The courtyard was bare. How late was she?

She barged into the classroom, out of breath. Instantly, the apology she'd prepared for her teacher died in her throat.

Every desk was filled. Jeannine Tremblay sat in Elka's chair, looking smugger than ever. Not one student sat on the floor. The class was half its normal size. No Ziggy or Felix…or Mademoiselle Bellegard.

A blond woman stood at the blackboard. Her stare was as cold as Jeannine's. She eyed the winded girl in the doorway.

"You're one of Francois's, *non*?" She didn't wait for Elka to respond. "I believe your class has gathered in the orchard. *Excusez moi…*"

She flicked a dismissive hand at Elka, who took a step back and bumped into the door jam. Jeannine and Romilly snickered.

Elka hurried behind the school, where blue crocuses and buttercups blossomed like popcorn. Their blooms should have brightened her, but her mind reeled. Maybe the school hired a new teacher to assist. Well, if so, she was grateful she still had Mademoiselle Bellegard, and not that surly blond woman.

She scanned the vast lawn. When she spotted the other children by a cherry tree, she sighed with relief. But as she came nearer, she saw their sullen faces. Even Monsieur Francois's normally jolly expression was sober. His body was stooped, like a wilted flower.

Mademoiselle Bellegard was nowhere to be seen.

Elka was too desperate for answers to be embarrassed by her lateness. "What's going on?" she asked, then hastily added: "Sorry I'm tardy, Monsieur."

Francois gave her a sympathetic smile. "Quite alright, Elka. I hope…" He glanced at the schoolhouse. "I hope you didn't have a hard time finding us."

"The new teacher told me you were here." She tugged on her ponytail. "Where's Mademoiselle Bellegard?"

Hettie sniffled. "She's gone."

Elka felt the blood drain from her face. "Gone? What do you mean?"

"Unfortunately, Mademoiselle Bellegard has been let go from her position. There was a...disagreement between her and a few of the other students' parents. Sadly, they could not reconcile their differences."

Greta buried her face in her hands. Next to her, Peter wiped his wet nose with his sleeve. Felix placed a hand on each of their shoulders and pulled them close.

A hot rush of emotions consumed Elka: rage, disbelief, confusion. She turned to Ziggy, who looked as dejected as she'd ever seen him. He raised an eyebrow but said nothing.

Now she understood perfectly.

The Pétain rally. Mademoiselle refused to force them to go, and Commander Tremblay got her fired.

Did Jeannine's stupid tantrums have anything to do with this? She'd always been jealous of Elka for getting more of Mademoiselle Bellegard's attention. Furious, Elka opened her mouth—but Ziggy nudged her, and she snapped it closed. Monsieur Francois had no idea she and Ziggy knew about the commander's visit. If she mentioned the rally, they'd be found out.

Francois explained the school's shortage of teachers, that parents complained of overcrowding. "I've decided we'll continue your lessons at the chateau." He gave the kids a tired grin, pretending this was a choice. "I'll instruct when I can, as will the rest of the grownups. But as you all know, our staff is quite busy already. That's why I'm hoping a few of you will assist with the primary classes."

"We're happy to help," Felix volunteered.

Ziggy nodded. So did Hettie and some of the older girls. Elka fixed her gaze on the grass at her feet. Of course, she would help. She wouldn't have to bear Jeannine's needling anymore, either. But she wasn't a teacher! She was a student. She belonged in school. What about her French lessons, the ones she did on the blackboard before class? The ones Mademoiselle Bellegard made just for her.

Reality set in like a cruel prank. Her beloved teacher, who'd been the closest thing Elka had to a parent in four whole years, was *poof!* gone. No goodbye—it was so unfair. She'd never again see Mademoiselle's lovely smile in the morning. She'd never again trace her perfect cursive on the chalkboard, repeat her words aloud and try to match her lilting French accent.

Hot tears burned her eyes. She squeezed them tight. She imagined tutoring Greta on verb tenses, teaching Peter geography. Her role would be different now.

The night she fled Dresden a hole had formed inside her. Living at the chateau, she'd managed to sew it back up. So long as she didn't examine it closely, it was like it wasn't even there.

But now the stitches had ripped wide open.

9

Ziggy

The hike back for lunch might as well have been a funeral march.

Mademoiselle Bellegard was all Ziggy could think about. Her bravery, how she'd defied the commander. And yet, he'd gladly cheer at Pétain's parade if it meant keeping his teacher around.

Elka lagged far behind. New, darker shadows underlined her eyes. Worried about her twiggy appearance, Ziggy reached in his pocket for the piece of dry toast he'd smuggled at breakfast. He handed it to Elka, who pushed it away.

She scowled. "Why didn't you wake me up?" she hissed.

"I wanted to," he fired back. "But Hettie told me you had a nightmare."

She screamed like she was being tortured. Those were Hettie's words, her eyes round with fear. *We all have nightmares, but I've never heard anyone scream like that.*

Elka's pout deepened. "So what? It was a bad dream. I missed my morning run."

He held out the toast again. "You can make up for it tonight."

Ziggy was glad to have an excuse for Elka to sleep in. Her sallow skin was the color of newsprint. Maybe she'd gotten faster, but if she was exhausted all the time, did it matter?

Anger drained from Elka's face. Her shoulders sagged.

"Thanks," she said, taking the charred bread and cramming it in her mouth. "I'm thorry. I'm just upset about Mademoithelle."

Seconds of chewing passed. Then Hettie popped up alongside.

"David said he heard Mademoiselle was fired because of Commander Tremblay."

"Really?" Ziggy bluffed. "What about him?"

Hettie shrugged. "I don't know, except he threatened to do more than fire her."

"What?" Elka dropped her toast to the ground. She looked like she might be sick.

"They can't—"

"But *then* some men went to the police inspector's house and threatened *him*," Hettie went on. "His maid overheard it, and she's friends with Darcy, and David overheard Darcy telling Francois about it this morning. The men told the inspector if anything happened to Mademoiselle Bellegard, they'd come after *him*. The maid thinks the men were part of the Resistance."

A thrill of revenge rushed through Ziggy. He pressed his lips together as Hettie kept talking. But his thoughts were careening in another direction.

The Resistance threatening the inspector, Mademoiselle getting fired, Commander Tremblay showing up unannounced…traitors were all around them, but there were heroes, too.

◆━○━━○━━◆

The next few days were a murky haze. After a weeks-long dry spell, rainclouds swathed the sky as if the weather, too, was depressed by Mademoiselle Bellegard's departure. Ziggy, Elka, and Felix took turns schooling the younger kids. Ziggy discovered he liked teaching lessons. With a bittersweet pang, he appreciated Pa's passion for it. The reward of seeing Peter's eyes light up when he'd memorized his multiplication tables, watching Greta's reading skills flourish.

Elka kept training, and while she swore it made her faster, Ziggy didn't buy it. Instead of returning refreshed from a run, she pulled on her ponytail nervously, more preoccupied than ever. Her eyes straying to windows, always scanning the woods.

One evening as Ziggy waited for her to return, musing how to confront her, he heard voices outside. His heart beat out of his chest. So far, they'd been lucky with Elka's sneaking out. What if someone noticed she was missing? Should he fib and say he didn't know where she was, or would that make things worse?

The plain truth was that in all the times he'd sat here to be her lookout, he'd never worked out what he'd do if someone questioned him. He hadn't really believed they could be caught. And what would happen to them if they were?

Was he really that careless?

The voices grew faint, Ziggy exhaled. But when he heard a hearty laugh, he stiffened again. That was Georges' laugh. In the dimness of night, he barely made out his gym teacher, bidding someone goodbye.

Ziggy's first chance, since the day at the cemetery, to see what Georges was up to.

Elka would be gone another hour. He couldn't wait here and miss an opportunity to spy on Georges. If he was careful to track the time, he'd be back before she was.

His mind made up, he set his book aside. He scurried from the study to the hat rack, grabbed Darcy's gardening cap and slunk out the door. In front of him, he saw Georges' lean figure turn left on Avenue Florissant.

Ziggy pulled down his cap, walking as fast as he could. The time he and Elka followed Georges to the cemetery played back in his mind. They'd been stuck under the Volkswagen until nearly dusk, waiting for the officers to leave. He wondered if he was being senseless. Was it worth the risk, to satisfy his curiosity? The answer was yes. Whatever the outcome, he had to warn Elka.

He set his jaw, his eyes fixed on his gym teacher. This was more than curiosity; Ziggy knew that Mademoiselle

Bellegard had been removed. The commander of the local militia had breached the chateau. All the time he and the other orphans had been in Annemasse, he knew they were swimming in shark infested waters. And now, the sharks were circling.

If Georges Loinger was a shark, he needed to know so that he could alert Francois of the danger. Francois couldn't protect the children in his charge forever, but Ziggy could at least help him buy time, before tragedy struck.

He ducked into an alley on Rue du Chablais. The street bustled with harried mothers pushing prams, businessmen sipping espresso at outdoor cafes, and couples out for an evening meal. He was grateful for the crowd; it was easier to blend in. From the other side of the avenue, he watched Georges enter a shop with suited mannequins in the display window.

Was Georges just shopping for a suit? Had Ziggy followed him for nothing?

Then he read the sign over the shop's entrance: *Deffaugt's Fine Apparel*.

The name took a second to register. Then it came to him…Jean Deffaugt, mayor of Annemasse! Ziggy remembered how warmly he'd greeted Georges when they first arrived at the welcome center. He'd been waiting there for them...and talking to Commander Tremblay.

What if the commander was in the shop, too? What if Ziggy encountered a roomful of French militia who might as well be Nazis?

He turned to leave—but he stopped himself. Retreating with more questions than answers was unthinkable. Plus, there was the Sports Festival: the event was next week, and he was puzzled by the whole thing. Was it a trap of some sort? The unsuspecting children in the chateau would be easily overtaken by enemies.

He *must* know if this danger was immediate, so he could help Elka—and Felix and Greta and Peter and the rest. It was too late to rescue his father, but this time, he could prepare the others—he could sound a warning.

Lifting his chin, he crossed the street to Deffaugt's shop and pretended to admire the window display. No one paid him any mind. The store sign read CLOSED, the lights were dimmed. Doubtful the door was unlocked he grasped the brass knob—and was surprised when it easily turned. As he leaned inside the shop and looked around, he heard faint conversation coming from the fitting room.

"Medals, too," someone said. "You can't have a race without medals."

Ziggy left the door ajar and moved between the racks of clothes. Smack! He stepped on a fallen hanger; it slapped his ankle like a fly swatter. Pain shot up his calf.

"Ow!"

Oh no. Had they heard him? Forgetting the throb, he squeezed between a row of fancy wool jackets. He pulled them together like curtains. He stiffened, cloaked in the fine, sweet-smelling wool, his pulse thrumming in his ears.

Ziggy held his breath. What was he thinking? He was in way over his head. Then the jackets abruptly parted, the chandelier's glare exposing his hiding spot. He squinted at the man fixed in front of him.

"Ziggy? What are you doing here?"

Georges. Instead of dread, a sudden boldness overtook Ziggy. He thought of all the people he had to save. He wouldn't let them down. He'd die first. He straightened his back, balanced on his good leg, then shuffled out of the rack. He adjusted his cap and looked up at his teacher.

"I followed you here, Monsieur," he said, his firm voice fueling the unexpected burst of courage. He would make Georges come clean. "Not only today, if I'm being truthful, but last week, too. When you led those children into the cemetery."

Georges' blue eyes creased in the corners. Somehow, he didn't look angry—maybe even…the opposite. "Is that so," he said, putting a hand to his chin. "Why don't you join us? This way, come along. It sounds like we have quite a bit to talk about."

Ziggy squared his shoulders and followed Georges into the fitting room. A mannequin dressed in lace layers posed in one corner. In another, a sewing machine sat atop a short pine table. Gray dress pants for a little boy Peter's age were folded over the back of a chair. Mayor Deffaugt perched on a stool, cradling a teacup. He let out a cough when Ziggy entered.

"Hello, young man!" He rose from his stool. "Looking for a suit?"

Georges laughed. He shut the door, turned the lock. "Not quite, Jean. This is Ziggy Wirth—he's one of my physical education students. Looks like he followed me here all the way from the chateau."

Pointing Ziggy to a folding chair, Georges took a seat on an overturned crate. He rested his elbows on his knees, leaned forward. Mayor Deffaugt lowered himself onto his stool.

"So, Ziggy." Georges crossed his sinewy arms. "Would you like to explain why I've found you in town, long after the chateau's curfew? And why this is the second time—so you tell me—you've snuck off?"

Ziggy's throat knotted. *Be truthful,* he told himself. *He already saw you. You have nothing to lose.* Even so, it was hard to forget that he was sitting in front of the mayor of Annemasse…and a possible Nazi accomplice.

He looked Georges in the eyes.

"Months ago…I overheard the two of you talking about the Sports Festival with no one else around. I thought maybe you were a spy. I wasn't sure if you were really staying with us to be our gym teacher. I mean… you're organizing a Sports Festival? When there's nothing but boiled potatoes to eat? Then Elk—" Ziggy caught himself, shook his head. "Then I…I couldn't sleep one night, so I took a walk in the woods and saw you meeting with another strange man. I heard the two of you making plans."

He waited for signs of rage on Georges' face. Seeing none, Ziggy went on. "I followed you both the next day. I saw you take some children—I'm guessing

Jewish children—into a graveyard...but they never walked out. What happened, Monsieur? What did you do to them? And what are your real plans for the festival next week?"

As Ziggy's words streamed out, Georges tapped his thumbs together. Mayor Deffaugt appeared tickled; his index finger hooked on the handle of his teacup. When Ziggy stopped talking, the two men swapped a look.

At last, Georges cleared his throat.

"Ziggy, I knew you were a clever boy. But even I underestimated you. So, I'm going to tell you the truth, and I trust you'll keep it between us." Georges took a deep breath. "I am indeed a spy...but for the *Resistance*."

Ziggy stared at him, not daring to believe it.

"As you're aware, the OSE instructed me to take you to Annemasse. Mayor Deffaugt has worked tirelessly to shield children like you. For me, this is a personal mission. When I was a boy, still a few years away from my bar mitzvah, I watched the German Workers' Party—that later became the Nazi party—grow in strength. When they rose to power and threatened my country, I enlisted in the French army. I—"

"Hold on. You mean you're Jewish?" Ziggy blurted. He must have misunderstood.

"I certainly am, yes."

This was amazing. Ziggy had never considered the possibility. It wasn't that he'd never met a Jewish person with blond hair or blue eyes. To Hitler and his followers, those "Aryan" physical traits were signs of perfection—they thought dark features were undesirable. But it hadn't occurred to him Georges might be Jewish.

That meant Georges was a target of the Nazis' hatred, too.

"As I was saying," Georges went on, "In 1940 I enlisted with the French military, then Hitler's army seized France. They captured me. But after a month in a prison camp, my fair hair and eyes aided my escape. I walked out, unnoticed. A year later, I was contacted by the OSE. They asked if I'd like to work for them."

Ziggy's awe grew, as did his guilt for being suspicious.

Georges had risked his life undercover, to help them.

"But what about the children in the cemetery?" he asked. "What happened to them?

Georges hesitated. "They're free," he finally replied. "And...no longer in France."

Ziggy rapid-fire pieced the puzzle together. The ladder propped against the graveyard wall. The Swiss border ran through the forest behind it. Switzerland was neutral territory where the war had no reach.

"You smuggled them into Switzerland?" he whispered.

"*Mon garçon*, you should know it's a group effort. My job was to lead them into the graveyard under the guise of a funeral, then help them over the back wall, into the woods, unseen. Another member took them over the border from there. It's..." He paused, his eyes shining and feverish. "It's much the same way I saved my wife and son. We hiked to Moillesulaz during the night. We parted before sunrise, and I haven't seen them since."

Ziggy was astonished by this news. "You've never mentioned your family before, Monsieur. You led them to the frontier between France and Switzerland? Did they make it to Geneva?"

"They took a tram there, yes—I know they're safe. And that's all that matters now."

He must miss them terribly, Ziggy thought. Yet here Georges was, protecting outcast children that weren't his own.

"I'm sorry," Ziggy said, ducking his head. "I should never have thought you were...that you might be..."

Georges put a calloused palm on Ziggy's shoulder. "Young man, never apologize for trying to help those you care about. I know it's hard to know who to trust these days. I must confess, you were right about one thing. I do have an ulterior motive with the Sports Festival."

Ziggy lifted his gaze. "You do? What is it?"

"For one thing, I want you—all of you—to experience joy. Even during these dreadful times." Georges sighed. "I know it's challenging. Sometimes it feels impossible. But we must have light in our lives. And secondly…"

He rubbed his hands together, like he was warming them over a fire. He cast a glance at Mayor Deffaugt, who set down his teacup.

"Nazi raids are taking place more and more frequently," the mayor told Ziggy. "I'm doing my best to prevent them from discovering us—discovering you—without giving away my role with the Resistance. But it's increasingly difficult. It's entirely possible, Ziggy, that…"

Mayor Deffaugt stopped mid-sentence. He coughed, picked up his cup and took a sip of tea. But Ziggy knew what he was going to say. He'd known it ever since he arrived in Annemasse.

"They're going to raid the chateau," Ziggy finished the sentence for him. "They're going to round up all of us, send us to camps in the east."

Georges' face fell. "Oh, child. How did you know about those?"

"I listen. I read. Grownups don't think kids know anything. But we do."

"Ah, I suppose that's right. There is so much darkness to know." He placed a hand on Ziggy's arm. "Whatever happens, it's vital you're all as robust as possible. Our training in gym will help prepare you for the worst."

Hearing Georges confirm his fears sent chills through Ziggy. His cheek twitched, his back tensed, but he tried to appear brave. After all, he told himself the same thing about Elka. Being fit could change her fate.

"I think our soccer training will be especially beneficial." Georges squeezed Ziggy's arm lightly, gave him a wink. Was Georges letting him in on another secret? He'd pried enough for now. "We have a few big games coming up after the Sports Festival. Trust me—it'll be fun."

He stood up. Ziggy rose also, too overwhelmed to mind his stinging ankle. He wanted to ask more questions, but Georges moved on.

"Mayor Deffaugt, I hope you're okay if we cut our meeting short?" Georges offered his hand to the mayor. "I'll be escorting Ziggy back to the chateau."

"Of course not," Mayor Deffaugt shook Georges' hand, then Ziggy's. "I'll be in touch soon. A pleasure to meet you, young man. My shop is always open if you need a tuxedo."

Ziggy grinned at the lighthearted teasing, but his mind swirled with all he'd learned. He wanted desperately to ask Georges about the soccer games—was he cooking up a scheme?

His curiosity overtook him as he and Georges made their way back to the chateau. "Is there something I should know? About the games we'll be playing?"

Georges shook his head. "It's not the right time. Soon. Trust me."

His gym teacher had trusted him with big, important secrets. Now he was asking for Ziggy's confidence in return. "Alright, Monsieur."

Kerosene lamps illuminated the front entrance of the chateau. "This outing will be classified, right?" Georges gave Ziggy another wink.

Ziggy smiled this time. "Yes, sir."

Then he made his way to the study, fast as he could, thankful Georges had turned in the other direction. He checked the clock—he'd been gone more than an hour, but Elka was still out running. Ziggy sat in the chair and gratefully propped his sore ankle on the footstool.

"Happy birthday!"

He nearly fell out of the armchair. From the doorway, a radiant Elka hugged a terra-cotta bowl in her hands.

"I planned it earlier this week," she said. "Darcy helped, but don't tell her I told you—she swore me to secrecy."

With that, she hurried over. She held out the bowl. Ziggy eyed a plump scoop of custard topped with blackberry preserves, like his mother used to make.

"I…" he was speechless. For the second time in as many hours. "I forgot it was my birthday today."

"Aw, no way. Really?" Elka set the bowl on the table, pulled a chair closer and settled in beside him. "You told me it was coming up a couple weeks ago, and Felix reminded me, too. Well, go on, try it. I know it won't be as good as your Ma's, but Darcy bargained for real cream and honey. Blackberry jam, too."

Ziggy knew he was blushing—he wasn't sure what to say. "Thank you," he mumbled, then picked up the spoon and took a bite. Sweet memories bubbled inside him like seltzer. He closed his eyes. The fresh cream, the syrupy honey, the tart burst of blackberries…he could hear his mother's tinkling laughter, hear his father's off-key singing of *Alles Gute zum Geburtstag*! He could see the glow of candles on a tall, buttery cake.

"Well? Is it good?" Elka asked eagerly.

Ziggy opened his eyes. "It's perfect. It's delicious."

He took another big spoonful, wanting to down the whole thing at once, but he resisted. He needed to savor this treat, share it with Elka, let it linger.

"We should talk to the staff about your bar mitzvah," she said. Elka sat back in her chair and tugged at a loose thread in the armrest. The fabric was worn off, leaving a feathery cushion poking through. "Have you mentioned it to them yet?"

Ziggy swallowed hard. The richness of the custard was making him feel sick—it was intoxicating and almost nauseating. "Why would I have a bar mitzvah?"

Elka's face dropped. "You're thirteen now."

"Sure, but...," he threw his arms up, the spoon still in his hand. "I can't have a bar mitzvah here. We're in hiding, Elka."

"I know that. I'm not saying we'd have the ceremony on the front lawn, but—"

"I don't want a bar mitzvah. I never want a bar mitzvah."

He tried not to think of what Pa would say if he could hear him right now. Or worse—if he could know his thoughts. Though his shame mounted, he couldn't control it. Because he wasn't mad at Elka for bringing up his bar mitzvah. He was angry at God.

"Okay," she softened, watching Ziggy dig into another bite of custard. Her eyes locked on him, but he didn't want to talk about bar mitzvahs or his birthday anymore.

He had something way more important to discuss. Something he'd also been sworn to secrecy not to tell. Something bigger than Darcy helping with a pudding recipe.

Licking the last bite off his spoon, he set the bowl down. "You'll never guess what I found out tonight," he began, and then he told her everything.

… 10 …

Elka

"I told you, we're safe here!"

"Shhh," Ziggy hushed. "Best keep this to ourselves for now."

He was right. Elka knew it. Georges was part of the Resistance! Between this, and the anticipation of the Sports Festival, she could barely contain herself. In a restless night of sleep before race day, her dreams swirled.

She chased Ruth through the forest, her sister's high-pitched giggles filling her ears. Elka called out her name but heard no answer; gnarled trees stood in her way. Their leafy tendrils dropped in burning heaps, but she ran on. She burst through a bramble of raging bushes, choking on the smoke—

Elka sat up in bed, breathing heavily. She rubbed her legs. Every limb of her body was tender and sore. Had her nightmare been real?

Then she remembered last night's run. She'd chased the shadow into a thorny patch, then tripped and fell. Ziggy had fetched ointment when she hobbled into the drawing room. After a cool bath, most of the swelling subsided. But now, every single cut and scratch pulsed with heat.

She needed sleep—real sleep, peaceful sleep, the kind of sleep she used to have before the shadow. She was fixated on the idea that Ruth was in the woods. Outside of the woods, at lunch or during lessons, she knew the whole thing was nonsensical. But in those hours she spent alone between dusk and dawn, with only the trees as guides—and nothing but the moon and stars lighting her path—anything seemed possible.

It was well past midnight and the race was in a few hours. She'd been training so hard.

When Elka got up in the morning, her joints ached. She splashed cold water on her face then walked groggily to breakfast. Ziggy waited with a dish of oatmeal. It looked like two servings, not the usual lukewarm lump in the bottom of the bowl.

"Sleep okay?" he asked.

Elka shoveled the porridge in her mouth. "Mm-hmm." She paused, eyeing him. "Where's your breakfast?"

"Finished it already."

"Oh." She kept eating. She suspected Ziggy was sneaking some of his food onto her plate. Part of her wanted to call him out, tell him he needed to eat, too. But she didn't want to embarrass him. He'd turned pink as a tulip when she made him custard for his birthday last week. It made her feel shy too, to see him blush like that.

After the meal, they strode to the field. It was a beautiful day, not a cloud in the sky, an ideal day for a festival.

The perfect distraction.

Ziggy said the festival was meant to keep their spirits up, even with the threat of raids. The way he explained it, the reason Georges trained them was to make them stronger. Fitness, their gym teacher said, gave them a chance of surviving the concentration camps.

The very thought made Elka shudder.

Honestly, as wonderful as it was to learn Georges was in the Resistance, she wasn't totally shocked. Even when she and Ziggy watched him leave the cemetery—without the children—she couldn't believe Georges was up to anything bad.

He had saved those kids. Right now, they were in Switzerland, safe from the Nazis, safe from raids, safe from the cruelty of the camps. They were free.

Elka would never in a million years say this to Ziggy, because she knew he would think it was foolish. But deep down, she believed that if Georges could save those children, he could rescue them, too. Of course, he couldn't sneak every orphan living here over a graveyard wall, but he would do what he could.

They were safe with him. She clung to that hope with all her might.

Along the grassy lawn, French flags flapped on rows of string. A canvas tent was staked. Leather mats, jump ropes, and burlap sacks were carefully arranged. When she saw it all, Elka's exhaustion turned into exhilaration.

Today would be unforgettable.

"*Bonjour*, Georges!" She and Ziggy greeted their gym teacher.

He smiled. But something was off. He was distant, lost in thought.

Then Felix jogged over. "Good morning," Georges addressed all three of them. "May I have a word with you?"

Skipping over the dewy grass, Greta and the other small girls picked up the jump ropes. They whipped them over their heads, tripping with every rope turn.

"I have…things to take care of," Georges said as Greta tumbled to the ground. "Can I trust you to lead the warmups and get things ready? Paint the finish line for the race?"

"What other things?" Elka's spirits dampened, but she tried not to show it. "I mean—whatever you need, Monsieur."

"Superb. I'll be back soon." Georges tipped his cap. Then he loped across the field and disappeared.

"I'll grab the paint can," Felix said. "Meet you two over there?"

"Sure." Elka turned to Ziggy once Felix was out of earshot. She cupped a hand over her mouth. "Do you think he's meeting with members of the Resistance?"

Ziggy chewed his lip. "I don't know. Maybe. Must be important if he's leaving before the festival begins."

For the next hour, Elka couldn't stop thinking about Georges. What was he up to? Was he in danger? What if he didn't return—should they go on without him? The thoughts rolled through her mind as she unrolled the tape measure to mark a 400-meter distance. Nearby, Ziggy pounded two rods into the ground, and hung a length of yellow ribbon between them.

Elka pictured herself running through the ribbon, snapping it free with her arms raised overhead. She glanced at Felix who seemed oblivious, at ease, playing with the children.

Most likely he assumed he'd win the race. It wouldn't be a big deal for him. But at this very moment, she wanted to win more than anything.

"You're ready," Ziggy said, reading her thoughts. "Tell me your plan again?"

"Sprint for two-hundred meters," she recited. "Slow

a few seconds to catch my breath. Then dash the last hundred, fast as I can."

"Concentrate on that, and nobody will beat you. I'll fetch more water. You should help Felix with the warm-ups—*les petites* are getting antsy."

Elka put a hand to her eyes, like a visor. In the farthest field, Felix wrestled a giggling Peter, and a few of his small friends. "Good idea."

As Ziggy headed to the well, Elka spotted Georges' megaphone on the grass and picked it up. It was heavier than she expected. She hoisted it with both hands.

"Ladies and gentlemen, it's the day we've waited for!" she shouted through the mouthpiece.

The children swarmed her like bees. Their noses were sooty, and dirt smudged their white shirts. Elka stood a little taller. Felix smiled.

"Form a circle, *s'il vous plait*. Same warmups as always. Greta, can you keep count?"

"Yeth!" Her pigtails bounced about her shoulders. After touching their toes for a ten-count, Elka lifted the megaphone again.

"Push-ups next!"

Everyone moaned. Ziggy approached, lugging two buckets. He teetered toward the tent, water sloshing over the lips of the pails, soaking his new shoes.

"Can you take over for a second?" Elka asked Felix.

"No problem." He lowered himself to the grass, then pushed up an extra time. He tilted his head and grinned. "This is my favorite part."

She rolled her eyes, then ran to Ziggy, reaching for a bucket.

"Let me help you."

He shook his head. "I got this. Save your energy."

She'd lost count of how many times he'd said that. It reminded her of Mama fluffing pillows to prop Papa's back as he hemmed garment after garment. Ziggy looked out for her, but he refused help for himself.

He was stubborn. That was for sure. But that was one of the things she loved about him.

She returned to the group of children, who romped on the grass like bear cubs. "What now?" Greta huffed.

"High knees—heels up!"

Watching from the porch, Francois's face glowed with pride at their performance. When he clapped his hands, the children stopped running in place.

"What do you say? Shall we begin?"

Kids scattered to their stations. Ziggy joined in, but his gaze strayed to the path alongside the chateau.

"Georges will be back soon," Elka assured him. But her belly ached. She'd heard stories of the Gestapo torturing Resistance fighters. It felt wrong to start the festival, but they didn't know when—or if—Georges would show up.

What if he *never* came back? Elka missed Mademoiselle Bellegard more than anything, and she couldn't stand the thought of losing another beloved teacher.

She pushed her worries aside as the festival got underway. Felix dominated games of four square with his forceful spikes. The three-legged race ended with Hettie and willowy Sophia crossing the finish line centimeters ahead of Peter and Greta, who got their legs tangled in knots at the last minute.

The sun climbed higher in the sky. Elka's nerves buzzed beneath its hot blaze. The 400-meter race was near. Her mind wandered to Georges and what he might be doing.

Finally, it was time for the contest. The smaller children gathered around the rugged track Felix had cleared with a push-reel mower. As Elka stretched out her calves to stay calm, Ziggy gave her back a light tap.

"Good luck," he said, then added, "not that you need it."

She flashed a faint smile. "Thank you, Ziggy. For… you know."

She tilted her head toward the woods.

"Make sure it was worth it," he winked.

She stuck her tongue out. He laughed and limped to the finish line, stopping every few steps to massage his hip. Taking a deep breath, Elka strode over to the start, where Felix, Sophia, and a few older boys took their places. Sophia was tall, but that was her only advantage. The other boys would go out too fast. At least that's what they did back at her running club in Germany.

She guessed Felix would start at an easy pace, then overtake everyone the last hundred meters. She believed her strategy—and her legs—stacked up against his. She took the lane farthest to the right, springing on the balls of her feet to warm up.

Felix wrapped a hand around his ankle, pulling it behind his back and reaching his free arm out for balance. He caught her eye and grinned.

"Good luck, Elka. Run fast."

She groaned and faced forward. Felix had to know how badly she wanted to win. She hoped he wouldn't go easy on her—slow down to let her cross first. Sometimes, he was too nice that way. She wanted to beat him for real.

"Looks like I'm just in time for the main event!"

Elka's head jerked at the familiar voice. She saw Georges, jogging across the yard, heading to the finish. She felt her balled up fists relax, but her stomach fluttered. Cries of *Go Felix! Go Elka!* encircled her.

This is it.

Elka crouched into starting position, with Felix on her left. She locked on the painted line, ignoring the whoops, the wind, the sun's glare—focusing only on crossing first.

The world paused. Georges lifted his arms. Elka's fingers trailed the gravel, her jaw clenched tight...

"On your mark...get set....go!" Georges dropped his arms, and Elka flew.

She pulled ahead, leaving everyone—leaving Felix—behind. She knew he would catch up in the second part of the race. Warmth flooded her body. When she ran cross country in Dresden, her family always came to support her at races. Even her mother, who pretended not to approve, would show up in her peacock-feathered hat and matching emerald-green gloves, one hand gripping Ruth's when Elka soared by.

She was weightless. No one could catch her, not even Felix.

"*Go, Elka, go!*"

Her pulse drummed in her ears. Her pace was steadfast, but her focus was broken. Because that deep voice, it sounded like Papa's.

Beads of sweat blurred her vision. Was that a brightly feathered hat near the flags? No, it couldn't be. *Focus, Elka.*

One-hundred meters to go. She realized she'd abandoned her plan—at the sound of her father's voice, she'd sped up, rather than pulled back. Too late now. All she could do was push to the finish line.

Her lungs were on fire. She pumped her arms, leaning forward, straining to hold pace. A long shadow appeared on her left, and Elka knew it was Felix, closing the gap. She glimpsed the finish line as it drew nearer, *focus, Elka, focus...*

And then the shadow of a young girl appeared on her right.

Elka yelped as she turned to look. The figure tore ahead, a hazy phantom careening faster than any human could run.

"Ruth!" she cried, her voice coming out choked and hoarse. Her muscles wailed in protest. She put on a burst of speed—she was so close Ruth was almost in her grasp—

—and then the world went black.

11

Ziggy

Ziggy could pinpoint the instant everything went wrong.

When Georges dropped his arms to signal the race start, Elka jumped out to the lead. Halfway through, Ziggy watched for her to throttle back, thinking *save it for the last hundred meters,* so she could out-kick Felix at the end. But she didn't slow down.

Felix caught her. He and Elka dashed in lockstep, both of them fixed on the finish. Then Ziggy saw her eyes drifting right. Her flushed-red face went ghostly white.

Everyone around him whooped and hollered, but Ziggy knew something was off.

He ran to catch Elka…even before she stutter-stepped.

With three meters to go, she collapsed on the track. Felix tore past, then looked over his shoulder as he broke through the ribbon. Georges hurried to Elka's side and put a hand on her clammy forehead.

Her eyes were wide open, but it was like she didn't see them.

Ziggy's heart pounded. "Elka? *Elka!*"

"She's breathing," Georges assured. "Felix! Water!"

Felix sprinted to the first aid tent. Sophia and the other runners crowded around her, but Georges shooed them away. "Step back. Give her space," he pleaded. "She's overheated."

Greta began to cry and Hettie comforted her. Ziggy gripped Elka's hand.

Wake up, he urged. *Elka, wake up.*

As if she heard him, she stirred. Her eyelashes fluttered like hummingbird wings.

"There, there," Georges soothed. "Breathe easy, *mon fille.*"

Felix appeared with a jug of water. He handed it to Georges. "I don't know what happened," he said, bending down so only Ziggy could hear him. "She was fine at the start. Then she really took off—I seriously thought she was going to beat me. And then…"

His voice quivered. He made a downward motion. Seeing Felix unnerved distressed Ziggy—he'd never seen him so distraught before.

Then Elka murmured something. Ziggy turned to her, and she blinked. "Roo," she said, lifting her finger, pointing in the distance. She struggled to sit up.

"Take it easy, now," Georges said. "Have some water."

He held out the jug, but she didn't seem to notice. She glanced from face to face, like she was looking for something. "Roo," she said again, her voice thick and drowsy.

"Elka." Georges handed the jug to Felix, who placed a finger underneath her chin. "Have something to drink."

Felix gently put the jug to her lips. Once she took a sip, he set it down. Slowly, the mob of kids fanned out. "How about we all go back to the games? I think it's time for the sack race."

Greta stopped sobbing. The children ran to the sacks on the other end of the field, and Darcy assigned teams.

"Good girl," Georges stroked Elka's knotted hair. "Take another little drink. Then we'll get you inside where it's nice and cool."

"Where—Where is *Roo*?" she muttered again, still dazed. "She was...here."

Ziggy frowned, confused. Who was here? He wobbled to his feet while Georges and Felix hooked their arms around Elka's and helped her up. "Roo," she mumbled again.

Then a light switch flipped on in his brain. *Ruth*.

She thought she'd seen her sister.

Hours later, Ziggy sat by the cot Georges had set up in the pantry. The whole thing looked odd: a girl sleeping next to the icebox, surrounded by pots and pans and bags of baking potatoes. But Darcy was right. The pantry was the coolest spot in the whole chateau.

The grown-ups were convinced Elka had suffered heatstroke. Ziggy supposed that was possible. They'd been outdoors all morning without a break, with the sun beating down. Plus, Elka spent every drop of energy on the race.

But why would she abandon her plan, after all her training? Why would she push harder, instead of easing back like she'd practiced? Now he knew the answer. She'd seen her sister on the track.

But Ruth hadn't been running beside her, which meant Elka was hallucinating. Maybe heat wasn't the only reason she was seeing things. True, she'd been a nervous wreck about the race for a week. Maybe something else was going on, too.

When she woke, Ziggy told himself *be patient*. Bombarding her with questions was a bad idea. Georges said to allow her to rest. But Ziggy needed to know where her mind had been before she'd fainted at the finish line.

Bewildered, Elka's eyes searched the room. She propped herself on her elbows.

"Brrr…the icebox sure works." She rubbed her bare arms, then looked at Ziggy. "So…I guess Felix won, huh?"

He sighed. Figured, she'd think of that first. "Yeah. But he said you might've beat him. I really think you would've if you hadn't…you know."

She pressed a washcloth to her forehead. "Yeah."

Although he knew he shouldn't, Ziggy pried for more details. "What happened out there? Why didn't you let up for a few seconds like you practiced?"

"I...I don't know. I guess I felt good. I thought I could sprint the whole way."

"It has nothing to do with thinking you saw Ruth?"

Elka's mouth fell open. "How did you—did you see her, too?"

"No, I didn't. Because she wasn't there. After the race you kept repeating her name."

"Oh." Her cheeks reddened. "I didn't...I mean, I know she wasn't actually there."

"Do you?"

He waited for Elka's response. "Look," she said at last. "You're going to think I'm—"

"I won't," he interrupted. "Elka, I've known something's up for the past month. You used to come back from your runs in a great mood. But lately, I don't know. It's like you've looked more like you've seen a ghost."

She shrugged. "Okay. The thing is...I see...my sister's shadow in the woods."

What? Ziggy shivered. He should've let her believe Georges could save them all.

"Have you...talked to her? I mean, the shadow?"

"No, no." She shook her head. "She's always...just ahead of me. At first, I wasn't even sure it was her. It was only this...this figure. I can't see every feature on her face, but I see her pigtails...." Her eyes filled with tears. She blinked them away.

"Oh-okay," Ziggy said unsteadily. "Maybe you trained too hard, right? Maybe you—"

"No, Zig, you're not listening!" her voice cracked. "Ruth is out there, and I need to find her. I can't let her go, not again."

Her pleading jarred Ziggy and his patience snapped.

"Elka, you have to know she's not here! She's been deported to a place where they treat her like a prisoner. Or worse. Same with your parents. Same with mine. We'll end up somewhere like that too, unless...the whole point of all this—the festival, your training—is to get stronger so you'll have a chance to survive. You know that, right? I told you what Georges said!"

Sorrow, then fury, flitted over Elka's face.

"We don't know *any* of that!" she said, her voice rising. "Especially about us! Georges told you he saved other kids from the raids. He's going to save us too—why don't you believe him?"

"He said the reason for gym class was to help us get as strong as possible, so we *might* survive."

"No." Elka crossed her arms. "You must be remembering wrong. There's no way Georges said that."

"You weren't there!"

"It doesn't matter!" she shouted. "Why would he rescue those children we saw in the cemetery and not us?"

"Because there's too many of us. It's kind of hard to make forty Jewish orphans vanish, like that." Ziggy snapped his fingers.

"Then Georges will find another way."

"You…you're imposs—" Ziggy shook his head and got to his feet. "Never mind."

"You know what's as important as physical strength?" Elka snapped. "Hope. Mademoiselle Bellegard taught us that. Or don't you remember?"

Ziggy glared at her. Had she overheard his conversation with their teacher that day? Despite the chilly temperature of the kitchen, he was flushed. He left the room without another word.

Hope was one thing. But did Elka believe her sister was alive? Four years ago, their families' lives were completely capsized and all were without life jackets to keep them afloat.

Now Elka thought she had a second chance to save Ruth.

She was chasing the impossible, and Ziggy had no idea how to make her understand that.

12

Elka

Elka didn't speak to Ziggy all weekend. Why should she be the first to apologize? What did she have to apologize for? Truth was, she'd been right all along, and Ziggy had been wrong. They could trust their gym teacher. He was with the Resistance. She wasn't sure how, but she believed Georges would help them escape.

She and Ziggy disagreed about many things, but that was alright—Elka could handle that. But Ziggy might as well have said she'd never see Ruth again—not ever.

She's been deported to a place where they treat her like a prisoner. Or worse. Same with your parents. Same with my parents. We'll end up somewhere like that too.

His words looped in Elka's brain, her emotions spun in circles. Anger, because Ziggy couldn't be sure any of what he said was true. Fear, too—what if he was right? But Elka also felt a bone-deep sorrow. Ziggy had been so selfless all these months. Spooning extra oatmeal in her bowl, staying up late to keep watch while she ran.

He believed she had a chance at survival.

But he didn't believe *he* had a chance.

The sad thought tugged at Elka like a current, until she circled back to anger, because it was easier to deal with than grief—and then the endless loop would start again.

She knew her parents and sister hadn't been at the race. *Of course*, she knew. But she'd seen her mother's feathered hat, her sister's braids tied with streaming ribbons. Did that mean something? Like maybe Ruth was out there somewhere, that she was okay? Elka decided that she had to be. She refused to give up hope.

Ziggy took to reading his books alone while he ate, so Elka sat with Hettie and Sophia. If they wondered why she was upset with Ziggy, they didn't ask. She chewed in silence while the other girls talked. She gazed out the window at the woods, longing for the solitude and freedom of the trails. But her collapse on the track had left her bruised. She needed time to heal. Besides, she couldn't very well ask Ziggy to stand guard while she snuck out.

No Ziggy. No running. No festival. Life at the chateau was becoming unbearably dull.

But Tuesday night, when a sharp, *rat-tat-tat* sounded from the front door, an uneventful life seemed like the best thing in the world.

Elka heard the knock while she and Hettie were at the washboard in the cellar. She dropped the wet blouse she'd been scrubbing, her hands white with suds. Something about the force, the authority of the rapping, caused her heart to leap to her throat. For the briefest moment, she smelled Mama's dumplings, felt Ruth's hand in hers, heard broken glass crunching beneath her feet as she fled, her father's half-finished tallis still clutched in her hands...

She whirled around and found herself staring into Hettie's terrified face. Neither spoke; there was no need. They knew what this was. They'd been waiting for it for four entire years.

A raid.

Ziggy! Suddenly, their fight seemed pointless. Elka had to find him.

She raced up the stairs, her legs quaking, with Hettie right behind. Elka gripped the banister, forcing herself to scale each step. The knocking came again, louder this time. Hettie let out a frightened whimper.

"Shh," Elka hissed, her hand on the knob. She opened the cellar door a crack.

She saw Monsieur Francois crossing the foyer. A moment later, there was the *click* of an opening door.

"Good evening! Can I help you gentlemen?"

He sounded so calm. For a fleeting second, Elka convinced herself there weren't Nazis standing on the porch. Maybe it was a door-to-door salesman with carpet sweepers to peddle. But when they replied, her blood turned cold. Colder than Jeannine's hard stare when she had to sit on the floor—before Mademoiselle was fired.

"Yes, sir. By order of the Vichy government, we'll be taking the children on this list."

Hettie gasped. Elka closed the door halfway, so only a sliver of light showed. Her view was scant, but she could hear every word.

"I see," Francois responded. "Well, of course I'll assist. Let me take a look here…oh, my, this handwriting is difficult to read, isn't it?" There was a long pause.

"These two here, Greta and Peter. In the infirmary with the measles. Highly contagious. Best to let them be for now."

This was met with an irritated sigh. "The other three, then?"

"Well, that's the thing," Monsieur Francois said, sounding baffled. "As I'm sure you know, I have over forty orphans here, but I make an effort to learn all their names. And I don't recognize a single one on here. Let me see...Felice Spiegel, ah, yes—she was transferred to another home last month. But Herschel Klein and Ezra Levy? I'm quite sure no boys by those names have ever lived here."

Hettie pinched Elka's arm so hard, Elka nearly squealed in pain. *Klein. Levy.* Her name and Hettie's were on that list. Monsieur Francois was pretending to misread them. Felice Speigel—that was Felix Speigelman. And of course, Greta and Peter, who didn't have the measles at all.

Elka's knees buckled. There were Nazi officers at Chateau Annemasse with a list that included her mispronounced name. The only thing standing between her and deportation was Francois's deliberate misreading. Would the men fall for it?

She wasn't about to stand here and find out.

Elka opened the door and coaxed Hettie to come with her. They fled down the hallway. When they reached the hearth room, she saw Felix directing the youngest children inside. He met her gaze, his eyes grim.

"Where's Ziggy?" she murmured. He nodded toward the window. Elka squinted to see past the lanterns, to the south lawn where fireflies winked. A dozen kids assembled by the garden. One began walking in her direction. She recognized his limp and sighed with relief.

Ziggy tottered inside, his face chalk white. When he saw Elka, his body rocked—then she threw her arms around him.

"My name is on their list," she whispered in his ear so the small kids couldn't hear. "Monsieur Francois is stalling, but what if they search the chateau?"

Ziggy hugged her quickly before pulling away. "That's why we're going out there," he said. "We'll hide in the forest until they leave. C'mon."

Steeling herself, she helped Ziggy and Felix herd the others down the knobby path into the woods. Except for the occasional sniffle and their shuffling feet, the children hardly made a sound. But how long could that last? There were so many of them and so many so young. If the Nazis searched the house and came up empty, wouldn't they hunt for them there? They'd be revealed so easily by the tiniest sound—a snivel, a snapped twig—and the soldiers would be upon them. Elka struggled with such fearsome thoughts as they walked further into the thicket. Maybe the Nazis would fall for Francois's trick and leave. Or…

Gah!! A strange man popped up and she nearly screamed. Ziggy reached for her hand. He held it tight.

The man stepped forward. Moonlight shone on his face and Elka felt a spark of recognition. He was young, with kind eyes, high cheekbones, and dimples in the corners of his mouth. Yes. She was certain she'd seen him before, right here in these woods.

"You're friends with Georges," she whispered. Next to her, Ziggy unclasped her hand. He released a long breath. She hoped he remembered him too, from the cemetery. She didn't want to say that aloud, and give away Georges' secret in front of the whole group:

This man was a member of the Resistance.

A wide smile lit up his face. He placed a finger to his lips, and just like that, the sniffling and whimpering stopped. He beckoned them to follow, and with Felix in the lead, everyone quietly obeyed.

He led them off the path and into a grove of trees. Eventually, they reached a clearing. Bowing at the waist, the man gestured them to sit. Bewitched by his hushed instructions, the kids sat on the ground. There was something about his manner that was so expressive, so mesmerizing, so graceful. Elka couldn't pry her eyes from him.

For the next half hour—or maybe longer, she lost track of time—the man captivated them with a show unlike any she'd seen before. The way he moved was like watching a real-life Charlie Chaplin, the silent movie star. Even without props, it was easy to "see" the invisible bucket of water he balanced on his head, the soccer ball he dribbled and kicked, the box he pretended to be trapped in. The younger children, some of their faces still shiny with tears, pressed their hands over their mouths to stifle giggles as the man dropped an imaginary dirt rake, only to step on the prongs and receive a prompt smack in the face. Peter looked like he might explode from holding in his laughter. His face turned a bright tomato red.

When another figure emerged in the clearing, Elka startled from her trance. Georges!

He counted them, one-by-one, and beamed. "I see you've all met my cousin Marcel." He put a hand on the man's shoulder. "Quite the talent, isn't he?"

Hettie spoke up in a shaky voice. "The gendarmes… are they still…"

"They're gone," Georges said. "I gave them a little tour of the chateau, explained the rest of you were busy with lessons. Then showed them off. I watched the car drive away myself. It's safe to return."

She broke into noisy sobs, and then Greta and Peter followed suit. Elka's body teetered, her hands trembled. It had been a close call. Such a close call.

"Come on," Georges said, motioning for the kids to follow him and Marcel. Elka hung in the back of the group with Ziggy.

"I'm sorry," she said.

He shot her a quizzical look. "For what?"

"Turns out you were right." A heaviness weighed on her now that her terror had subsided. "My name was on that list. I'll probably be sent away, just like…"

She couldn't bring herself to say her sister's name.

Ziggy took her hand.

"No; I'm the one who's sorry. *You* were right. Georges saved us, like you said he would."

Elka only nodded. Ziggy knew as well as she did that just because they were rescued tonight didn't mean they would be tomorrow or the next night, or the one after that.

Maybe it was out of their control and it was just a matter of time before the Nazis caught them. Maybe it was a matter of how long they had left before danger closed in around them.

13

Ziggy

The next morning, Felix roused Ziggy from a troubled slumber.

"What? What's wrong?" Ziggy asked, dizzy from sitting up so fast. Last night's narrow escape had left his mind spinning like a cyclone.

"Nothing. The others are asleep. Georges wants to see us."

"Huh? Why?" Ziggy threw his covers aside. "Never mind. I'll be ready in a minute."

When his feet touched the floor, a sharp pang seared his thigh. Huddling in the woods hadn't been good for his hip. But he wouldn't let Felix see him flinch.

At this painfully early hour, Felix was already dressed. He patiently waited for Ziggy to pull on his trousers and wash his face. As Ziggy brushed his teeth, he caught a glimpse of himself in the cracked mirror. His mustache was coming in thicker.

Asking Francois for a razor had embarrassed him. Ziggy didn't know how to shave.

"We're meeting in the storage shed out back." Felix paused and studied Ziggy's reflection. "It's really starting to come in, huh?"

For a moment, Ziggy didn't know what he was talking about. Then his face warmed. He straightened up and stroked the velvety hairs on his upper lip. "I guess so."

"Need a razor?" Felix asked as they headed downstairs.

"I haven't…I'm not sure how to…" Ziggy trailed off, hoping to change the subject.

"It's easy. I'll show you."

"You will?"

"Sure."

Ziggy exhaled. He'd learn to shave after all. A longing for his pa swept over him. No use trying to dismiss it. His mind wandered back to that Hanukkah celebration, six years ago, when his ma gave Pa the razor. When his parents danced to the music on the radio all night.

His eyes grew misty, thinking about them and the gold-embossed book his aunt had given him. He'd had to leave it behind in Berlin. But he was grateful for Felix's offer, and he was even more grateful that his friend didn't make him feel self-conscious about the whole thing.

Inside the shed, Georges met them with a hearty *bonjour*. Beside him, Elka was perched on a rough wood pallet. Dark circles punctuated her eyes. What was she doing here?

He imagined a dozen scenarios. She snuck out this morning to go on a run and Georges caught her. She told Georges her sister was in the woods and now Georges was seriously worried about her mental health. Elka was hurt, Elka was in trouble, Elka was—

"I'm sure you're wondering why I plucked you three from your beds at such an ungodly hour," Georges said. "Please settle in." Ziggy gingerly lowered himself on a stool. From her seat on the pallet, Elka rolled a soccer ball to-and-fro with her palm, and Felix remained standing.

Then it dawned on Ziggy, what this meeting was about. The Nazis would return and Georges wanted to warn them. Monsieur Francois's clever ploy, pretending to misread their names, could only work for so long.

He threw his shoulders back. Maybe if he looked courageous, he would feel it too. It had worked at Mayor Deffaugt's shop, so why not here?

"Let's get right to it," Georges began. "I'm sorry for last night's disturbance. Do you recall the day of the Sports Festival? When I left for a spell? I received an urgent call that morning—from the mayor. He informed me round-ups of Jewish children were—are—imminent… to further Hitler's desire to…" Georges hesitated, "…to dispel of every Jew."

The dusty air in the shed was stifling. Ziggy couldn't bear to look at Elka. It wasn't as if they hadn't known Hitler's horrifying plan but hearing it from Georges made it more real.

"As most of you know, I'm a member of the French Resistance," Georges went on. Ziggy glanced at Felix, wondering when Georges had told him the truth. "I hid this from each of you, along with many things—for your safety. But seeing you three last night, the way you took charge when the gendarmes arrived, instinctively gathering the others, keeping them calm, leading them into the woods…I decided it was time to tell you."

Pride swelled in Ziggy. Elka hugged the ball in her lap.

"I'm about to trust you with a very important secret." Georges' voice dropped an octave. "I have a plan for you—every child here, at the chateau—to escape. But I need your help."

Ziggy thought he'd misheard. He waited for Georges to correct himself, to take it back. But that one word rang in the air like a bell, reverberating in his ears.

Escape. Escape. Escape.

Elka's breathing shallowed. Felix appeared unmoved, except for the smallest twitch of a smile in the corner of his mouth.

"How?" he was first to ask.

Georges walked to an old chalkboard leaning against the wall. He picked it up and flipped it around. On the other side was a sketch of a soccer field, with circles representing different positions.

"A soccer game."

Georges pulled a piece of chalk from his pocket. He began to explain his strategy for the match. Ziggy listened, not daring to believe what he was hearing—the words suspended in mid-air, like apparitions. That one word still rang out like the echoes of a pealing bell, vibrating through Ziggy, filling him with something that, if he wasn't careful, might even turn into hope.

Escape.

14

Elka

Elka's weariness melted like hot wax. In fact, she felt like she could carry every single orphan over the Alps to freedom if she needed to.

Fortunately, Georges had a better plan.

"I've located a manicured soccer field on the edge of the woods, a few blocks from the cemetery," he explained. "From there, it's about two and a half kilometers through the forest to the Swiss border. The OSE members in Switzerland are making the necessary arrangements for us."

"But you said yourself, we can't escape the way those other children did," Ziggy interrupted. "There are too many of us. If Nazis are patrolling, won't they notice a whole soccer team has gone missing?"

"Indeed, they would," Georges agreed. "Which is why I've developed this playbook." He drew several intersecting lines on the chalkboard. Elka leaned so far forward, she almost fell over. "We'll play a regular game of soccer for the first half, so as not to arouse suspicion. Ziggy will be right defender and Elka will be left defender, while Felix will be center forward. In the second half, you will execute this play—" Georges scribbled X's and O's on the board. "Felix will pretend to go for a goal, but he'll send the ball Elka's direction. Elka will attempt to pass to her team's forward, but the ball will go out of bounds...*here*."

Georges sketched a long line, representing Elka, from the circle to the scribbled forest. Then he turned to face them.

"Elka, you will retrieve the ball and toss it to Felix but remain out of sight in the woods. Another player will take your place. Felix will go for another goal, instead sending the ball to Ziggy, who will execute the same strategy as before. Once his replacement is on the field, Felix will kick the ball out of bounds a final time and toss it to Sophia, who will take his spot as center forward while he joins you two. Marcel will meet the three of you and guide you to the border."

Elka's body tingled as she pictured it. Running through the woods, like she had so many times. Only this time, there would be no halfway point…no marker to turn around. She would keep going and going until she got to the Swiss border. Beyond the Nazis' reach.

She would be free. But…

"Wait," she said, frowning. "What about the others? Hettie, Greta, Peter, Sophia…"

"As Ziggy pointed out, it would be far too suspicious for an entire team to vanish," Georges explained. "After you three are gone, we'll finish the game and return to the chateau. Then the next week, we'll head back to the field and play another game. And another.

"In fact, yesterday, a new group of children arrived in Annemasse by train, and I have hopes to help others. We'll add team members to replace those who've left—until everyone has crossed to safety."

It was brilliant. Elka knew it, and yet—she'd left her sister Ruth behind once before. A knot formed in her throat. No way would she leave the younger children this time, too.

Felix shook his head. "Shouldn't we begin by saving the little ones? I prefer to stay behind, make sure *les petites* go over the border fence before I do."

Elka nodded fiercely. "Me too," she said.

"And me," Ziggy added.

Georges sighed deeply. "A noble offer by you all. But I've given this a great deal of thought. Our strategy doesn't only require strong soccer skills, but also good acting. You must look the part of carefree children playing a game, not orphans running for your escape. Not to mention if the other children see the three of you pull this off, they'll feel more confident. Which will increase their chances of success. Also," he said, his blue eyes widening, "this plan is risky. Capture is possible. Your bravery is why I feel the three of you should be first to attempt it."

Elka's chest tightened. Felix nodded his head.

"That makes sense," he said. "In that case, I'm ready. Let's do this."

"And me," Ziggy agreed somberly.

Elka bit her lip. *I can't leave first. Not again.*

"Excellent, it's done then," Georges said. "Now, I'll need your assistance training the others. This will be a bit tricky. For one thing, the fewer people who know a secret, the more likely it remains one. That's why we should hold off on letting the other children in on our playbook, until before the first game."

Then Elka remembered Greta was up all night, weeping into her pillow. Hettie's face was the color of a bleached sheet when they returned from the woods. Elka wanted to tell them things would be okay. But she couldn't stand the thought of abandoning them. She would talk to Ziggy—maybe he could help her convince Georges they should escape last.

"One final thing," Georges said, turning directly to her. "We'll train hard for this…but not *too* hard. You're a great runner, Elka. But we need you in tip-top shape, okay?"

It might have been her imagination, but she thought Georges gave her a little wink. Was he talking about her blackout at the Sports Festival? Or did he know about her training runs? It took all of her willpower not to trip on her words.

Even when she replied simply, "Yes, sir."

"Good. Then let's go over our plan again."

Georges picked up the chalk. Elka's heart hammered like she'd run from here to the border. She watched as Ziggy stood—his knee slightly bent—and limped to the board.

He tapped out lines and circles, but Elka's mind raced, and she couldn't concentrate. *Can't the younger kids be first to leave?*

"Elka?"

Startled, she looked up to see Felix. He stooped to hand her something. In his outstretched palm she saw a round gold medal hanging from a blue ribbon.

"What…" Elka looked up at him. "Is that the medal you won at the festival?" She brushed her thumb over its tarnished surface. Though she'd wished for one, she'd never seen medals laid out for the race.

"This was Georges' medal first," Felix said softly. "He was a talented runner like you when he was younger. He gave it to me after the race. But…." Felix paused and ran a hand through his shiny red curls. "I want you to have it. You ran an incredible race, Elka. You deserve this. I was sure you were going to win."

He placed the medal in her open hand. It was cool to the touch, and she held it tightly. "Felix," she whispered, "Thank you."

Felix smiled, then he turned back to Georges and Ziggy. Elka tried to listen also, but the squiggles on the board blurred like a shadow.

If she really stood her ground, maybe they'd agree to *her* plan.

For the first time in years, she felt like things might be all right.

15

Ziggy

The next two weeks roared on. Gym class switched over to full-time soccer practice. Afterward, they ran laps around the field. Most of the kids loved training, even as it ramped up and their legs grew tired and stiff. In a few more days, they'd play real matches.

Ziggy remembered what Georges said in Mayor Deffaugt's store. *Whatever happens, it's vital you are all as robust as possible. Our training will prepare you for the worst.*

If their strategy unraveled, if they were rounded up like cattle—at least they'd be strong.

Physical strength wouldn't keep them all from suffering. But something changed in Ziggy, listening to Georges' scheme in the shed before sunup. Strength of spirit, he realized, was even more powerful.

A scene took shape in his head. A vision of him, Elka, Felix—together in a small town in Switzerland, free to walk the streets without fear. He'd done his best to squash the image, but it sprouted uncontrollably, like a field of wildflowers.

Elka said she believed Georges' soccer game would work. But it was what she wasn't saying that bothered Ziggy. He couldn't put his finger on it, but she was holding back. He could see it on her face, a hint of sadness, when they talked of their escape.

Anyhow, he didn't have the heart to tell her how easily things could all go wrong. At least she'd listened to Georges' advice about not over-training. The dark circles under her eyes faded, color returned to her cheeks. And Ziggy vowed he'd never mention Ruth again. Yet while Elka didn't speak her sister's name either, he saw her gazing into the woods at practice.

Another week of training passed. Then one morning, when the sticky air clung to their sunburned skin, Georges asked the children to form a circle. Ziggy sat next to Elka, swatting at a fly that landed on his outstretched shin.

This was it. Georges was about to fill everyone in on their escape plan.

Which meant they'd carry it out soon.

"Boys and girls. Tomorrow will be an extra-special day," Georges began. "We'll play our first official soccer match!"

Everyone hooted—except for Ziggy, Elka, and Felix. When Ziggy shooed the fly again his arm brushed Elka's, and he thought he could feel her pulse racing with his.

"This will be no ordinary match," Georges went on. "In fact, we'll practice some challenging new plays."

In spite of his nerves, Ziggy couldn't stop smiling. He'd drilled dozens of times with Elka and Felix over the past couple weeks. Once or twice during each practice, one of them would "accidentally" kick the ball out of bounds. Or to the other team's defender. They'd gotten pretty good at pretending they were going for a goal, while aiming in another direction entirely. None of the other kids had caught on yet.

He hoped the officers patrolling the field tomorrow would fall for it, too.

As Georges explained their game plan, Ziggy looked at Hettie and Sophia—they were mesmerized. "First

Elka, then Ziggy, and last of all Felix will sneak into the woods while the match goes on," their teacher said.

Next to Ziggy, Elka tied and untied her boot. She took it off and shook out the pebbles.

"You must continue playing while they hide," Georges went on. He gave the younger children a stern glance. "Think of this as hide-and-seek but with one big difference. Elka, Ziggy, and Felix are all on your team. You don't want to give away their hiding spot, so don't peek."

Greta glowed. Hide-and-seek was her favorite game on rainy days. But Ziggy was struck with the memory of her on the train ride all those months ago, staring wide-eyed into the face of a Nazi guard. That turned out okay, but at the time it was a white-knuckler.

For the millionth time in the last two weeks, a swell rose in his chest. Could they really pull this off?

Georges blew on his whistle to end the meeting. Practice began and Felix feigned a goal kick, then booted the ball out of bounds into the woods. As he raced after it, Greta watched him and giggled.

"Stop looking, Greta!" Peter hollered from the opposite end of the field. "He's *hiding*!"

Everyone laughed—except Elka and Ziggy. Even Georges chuckled a little. "Don't you think yelling *he's hiding* might give away Felix's hiding spot too?"

Peter hung his head. "Sorry, Monsieur."

"Don't worry," Georges assured. "That's what practice is for. Let's try that play again."

The kids took their positions. Felix returned to the field and this time, when he kicked the ball away, Greta faced the opposite direction. Even so, Ziggy could see her shoulders shaking with laughter. *Well, it's a start*, he thought.

After an hour of this, the children quit giggling each time Felix vanished into the woods. They promptly resumed play whenever he tossed the ball to Elka. Ziggy went for a goal kick next. In spite of his sore hip, his aim was perfect. His right leg was so strong, the ball sailed ten meters outside the foul line. When it was Ziggy's turn to throw the ball to Elka, he hid behind a tree then waited for her to make the same move. Moments later she appeared at his side, sweaty and breathless. She wiped her forehead with the back of her hand but hardly looked at him.

"You okay, Elka? You seem kind of zapped today," he told her.

Elka ignored him. "They're already playing again," she said quietly. "This is going better than I thought. Sophia took my spot like she's supposed to."

Ziggy slowly exhaled. Elka was right, things were going smoothly. A few meters away, from the cover of a cherry tree, Felix gave them a thumbs up. When Georges trilled his whistle, the three of them jogged in to join the rest of the team.

"Outstanding work today, all of you," said Georges. "I'm convinced we're ready. Yes, Peter? You have a question?"

Peter kept his arm raised. "What happens after tomorrow?" he asked, his high-pitched voice rising. "Will we still play soccer during gym?"

Ziggy peered at Elka. Her expression reflected his guilt ten-fold. They would be first to go, like Georges instructed. Was that why she looked so out of sorts?

"Not only will we continue to train," Georges replied, "we'll play the same game. Everyone will get their turn to hide."

A grateful ripple passed through them. Ziggy knew the others were picturing it, too: that moment in the forest when they'd stay hidden until it was safe to move, then make their escape. There was no way not to see it. Right there, in front of them.

"I need more practice," Peter piped up again. "What if I can't kick the ball all the way to the trees?"

"I'll help you," Felix offered. "I'll play keeper and you try to score a goal on me. Let's stay outside and work on it, okay?"

"Yes!" Peter jumped up and down. "Please!"

"What a splendid idea," Georges encouraged. Felix and Peter trotted back to the field. "Everyone else, class is dismissed. We'll head to the pitch tomorrow at ten sharp."

Ten sharp. Ziggy walked away in a daze, oblivious to the chatter around him. At ten o'clock tomorrow morning, they would leave the chateau forever.

It might have been Ziggy's imagination, but the stew at dinner that night seemed to pack more meat than they'd had for months. He gobbled huge spoonfuls, wondering if Darcy did it on purpose—a farewell dinner of sorts. As thrilled as he was about the possibility of escape, the idea that he might never again see Francois, Darcy, and the rest of the staff gave him unexpected pangs of sadness.

"I don't know how I'll possibly sleep tonight," Elka said, stirring her stew thoughtfully. "I wish I could go on a run to clear my head, but I want to rest up for tomorrow."

Ziggy swallowed another mouthful. "Should we go outside and see how Felix and Peter are doing? Maybe drill some more?"

"I'd like that," Elka said. "There's something else I need to talk to you about, too."

"I'm all ears. Let's go."

The two of them picked up their bowls, scraped them clean and set them in the dish tub. Then, before Darcy could assign them last-minute kitchen duty, they slipped out the back of the chateau. The sun was a glowing red sphere, ducking behind the mountains.

"I'll get us a ball," Elka shouted, jogging to the shed. "Meet me at the field."

Woof...woof! Woof woof woof!

The sound of a growling dog stopped Ziggy in his tracks. Elka, too. More than a soccer pitch away, they saw a tall-eared German Shepherd, tugging on his lead. A uniformed soldier held the other end of the leash. He yanked on the snarling dog's collar and pointed at Felix.

Allez bouge-toi!

That's when Ziggy spied Peter, cowering under an evergreen. His face was buried in a heap of pine cones that had fallen to the ground.

Suddenly, his heart leaped into his throat. "Elka, go back inside!"

"No, no...no way," she refused. "We—we need to help them!" Instead of heeding his plea, she bolted by Ziggy, who trotted as fast as he could toward Peter. Elka reached the boy first, and he hugged her tight.

Then the three of them watched in horror as the soldier handcuffed Felix.

"Please...please Ziggy—Elka— take Peter and run!" Felix cried out as the dog snapped at his heels. He shook off the gnashing canine, but the soldier pushed him onto the back of a truck with the butt of his rifle.

The shepherd leaped in the truck bed. Then the officer sped off over the grass and onto the gravel road, tires spitting rocks in every direction.

As the truck taillights faded from sight, Ziggy felt completely helpless...like he was standing at the bottom of a well, with no way to climb out. Finally, he willed himself to move. He put an arm around Peter and pulled him close.

"C'mon. L-let's get you inside," he said in a shaky voice. When the three of them shuffled in—Peter whimpering like a frightened animal—a hush descended on the dining hall.

Hettie plunked down her fork and pushed her chair back. She hurried to the door as fast as she could where Elka blocked her way.

"Stay here," Elka begged her.

Monsieur Francois knelt in front of Peter, who now wept so hard he couldn't speak. A wave of doom swept through Ziggy, like it had when his pa was arrested. His heart punched its way out of his chest. He knew what Peter would say next, and none of it was true.

"I-it's my fault!" the boy bawled. "We went in front to practice k-k-kicking because it was t-too dark out back. I d-didn't see the soldier until I kicked the ball in the street. He saw me…he saw us…and Felix told me to hide and then—"

Peter crumpled in a heap. Ziggy saw the color drain from Elka's face. He pinched himself. Maybe it was all a bad dream. He pictured Felix—strong, stoic Felix—striding out to meet the officer, distracting his attention from Peter. The very night before he would have made his escape, Felix sacrificed himself to save another child.

Now it was too late for him.

16

Elka

Elka lay awake in her bed past midnight, listening to the soft crying of the girls, but her eyes remained dry. She was too stunned, too angry for tears.

Fate was cruel. Felix was supposed to be asleep in the boy's dormitory right now. He was supposed to eat breakfast with her and Ziggy like always, teach lessons one last time with them, walk to the soccer pitch with them. Play the game with them.

Escape to Switzerland with them.

But Felix was gone.

Elka couldn't do this, she couldn't lie here and listen to Greta's sniffles one more second. Squirming out from under her covers, she tiptoed into the dark hallway.

"Elka?"

Startled, she turned around. Ziggy sat, his back against the wall, outside the boy's dormitory. His right leg was bent at the knee, the left one straight out on the floor. Elka joined him. She slumped down the wall and hugged her knees to her chest.

"I couldn't spend another second in there," she said.

"Me either. I haven't hurt this much since they took Pa."

Elka looked up but Ziggy didn't meet her gaze. He rarely spoke about his parents, and never talked about the last time he'd seen them. What felt like hours of silence passed—though it may have been less than a minute—before he spoke again.

"They came in while Ma was cooking. Threw a few punches at Pa, he didn't put up a fight. His glasses fell off, and one of the men stomped on them, hard. They laughed."

Elka closed her eyes. *Steaming dumplings. Ruth's sweaty hand. Running over broken glass, clutching a half-finished prayer shawl.*

"When they took him, Ma and I ran—I could run faster back then. Not as fast as you, but the special shoes I wore made it easier. We ran to old Frau Wagner's house across the street. She wasn't Jewish, so Ma knew they wouldn't come barging into her house. Frau Wagner, she saw the whole thing through her window. She let us in, rushed us upstairs." Ziggy paused. "We spent eight months in her attic."

Eight months. Elka tried to wrap her mind around it. Eight months in a stuffy space the size of a tinder box. No grass or breeze, no music or laughter. No talking above a whisper.

"She did her best to feed us, but Frau Wagner didn't have much to begin with," he went on. "She gave me books, too—to keep up with my studies. Then one day she fell down the stairs after bringing us supper. Messed up her hip. Ma snuck out for our groceries after that. She was at the market when a couple of men said she 'looked like a Jew' and beat her. Ma's nurse friend stitched her up. She's the one who told Ma about the OSE."

A warm tear trickled down Elka's cheek—it dropped from her face to the floor.

"Ma knew we couldn't live in that attic much longer. Not with Frau Wagner laid up like that," Ziggy said.

"She got to a telephone booth and called the number her nurse friend gave her. The very next day I left the attic—for the first time since Pa was taken. I'd outgrown my shoes. The walk to the train station was hard because I hadn't been getting much exercise. Ma put me on the train to Versailles. I didn't..." His voice broke. "I know this sounds dumb, but I was so confused, I didn't realize she wasn't getting on the train with me...until it was pulling away. I watched her standing on the platform. She was crying and crying. She knew she'd never see me again, but I didn't...I didn't realize..."

"I understand." Elka gulped. "I didn't either when I...when I ran away. When I left Ruth."

Ziggy was silent for a long moment. "Elka, do you still believe in God?"

She was stunned. Not just at the question, but at the fact she'd never considered it before. "Yes," she said, after some hesitation. "I do. Do you?"

"I don't know." Ziggy let out a humorless laugh. "Maybe, I'm not sure anymore. Pa paid a tailor to sew a tallis for my bar mitzvah when I was nine. Can you believe that? That's how excited he was about it."

"That's really sweet," Elka said softly. She remembered Ziggy's words on his birthday. *I don't want a bar mitzvah. I never want a bar mitzvah.*

"He heard about a really good tailor in Dresden. Even paid him an advance for his work," he went on, shaking his head.

Elka blinked. "In Dresden?"

"Yeah."

A strange vibration began in her chest, zipping under her skin as she got to her feet.

"Ziggy, wait right here," she said, hurrying back into the dormitory.

17

Ziggy

Ziggy leaned the back of his head against the wall. He closed his eyes. He couldn't stop thinking about Felix, and Pa, and Ma. All the sacrifices they made to protect others. But they shouldn't have had to do any of it. Felix should be heading off to university, not a prison camp. Ma and Pa should be with Ziggy, all together as a family.

Halevai…I wish it were so…

He heard Elka's feet padding down the hall, but he didn't bother opening his eyes. He was tired of talking about his father.

"I took this, the night the Nazis came for us," she whispered. She paused, waiting for Ziggy to look, but he didn't. Maybe he couldn't. "My father was half-done sewing it. It's the only thing of his, of any of theirs, that I have left."

Curiosity won out. He opened his eyes. He stared down at the ragged, messy underside of a prayer shawl, then peered up at Elka. Her eyes glistened in the dark corridor.

"Papa used to say sometimes life was like this," she said, tracing her fingers over the bumps and knots, the jagged stitches that rippled across the tallis. "Like the underside of a tapestry. It doesn't make sense—not until you turn it over."

Carefully, like she was handling crystal, she turned it to the other side. It was shimmering, magical. Ziggy sat motionless, unable to breathe.

"This is the big picture," she said. "The grand plan, where all that jumbled mess on the other side makes sense. You just have to see it."

With an unsteady hand, Ziggy reached out and touched the tallis. The stitches were smooth and silky beneath his fingertips, and up close, he saw how intricate the pattern was: several shades of blue thread mingled with gold and gray and cream. A question bubbled inside him. Could it be? It couldn't possibly be.

Could it?

"Your father," Ziggy said at last. "You told me...he was a tailor. Right?"

Elka nodded. "A tailor in Dresden."

It couldn't be. He tried telling himself there were a hundred Jewish tailors in Dresden. The chance his Pa selected Elka's father four years ago to make his tallis was impossibly low.

Yet, as he pressed his hand against the fabric, the strangest, most wonderful sensation began to spread through him. It was almost like music, the opening notes of an uplifting melody starting in his chest and trickling outward.

This was the tallis his father planned to give him for his bar mitzvah. He knew it in his soul, knew it as surely as he knew one plus one equaled two. It had been years since he'd experienced this sensation and it took him a few moments to find the word for it.

Faith.

18

Elka

For once, Elka's sleep was free of nightmares.

In her dream the final night at the chateau, she ran. She wasn't chasing the shadow of her sister. Nor was she fleeing men with red armbands and bayonets. She ran for the pure joy of it, dipping under the arches of foliage, the tallis around her shoulders flying like a cape behind her.

When the first ray of sunlight brushed her face, she woke up. She remembered watching Ziggy take the tallis in his hands and the look of wonder on his face. She'd insisted he take it back to the boys' dorm with him. They would never know for sure if their connection began four years before his arrival at the chateau.

But she believed. And so did Ziggy. That was all that mattered.

It wasn't until Elka spotted Felix's empty seat in the cafeteria that sorrow knocked her senseless. She tripped in the doorway, dropping her tray.

"Are you okay?" Ziggy stood up from his seat at their usual table.

She sat down opposite him, held her head in her hands. "Felix," was all she could say.

Ziggy shook his head. "I know, same here. I don't want to feel excited for today. Not when Felix is… wherever he is." He pushed his bowl of porridge aside. "It makes me feel awful in a way, but when I woke up this morning, I thought of the tallis, and the soccer game, and the chance that in a few hours we could be…" He stopped. "Then I thought about Felix. He's supposed to be with us."

Elka stirred her porridge half-heartedly. She knew she needed to eat, but guilt and grief, missing Felix, made her stomach hurt. The reality, the *finality* of everything was sinking in. This would be her last meal at the chateau. No more washing dishes with Hettie, no more chasing after Peter when he brought a toad inside from the garden. No more helping Greta read from her first chapter books, reciting the words out loud with her when she got to the last page.

The children filed outside, where Georges was waiting, along with Monsieur Francois and Darcy. She could tell from Georges' face that Francois had shared the sad news.

Once the kids gathered, Georges split the silence.

"Everyone here has suffered terrible losses," he said. "Our mothers, fathers, brothers, and sisters. Grandparents, aunts, uncles, cousins. Last night, a dear friend was stolen from us, too."

A lump rose in Elka's throat as he spoke.

"Felix is strong and courageous. He is a survivor. And so is each one of you. That is exactly what Felix would tell you if he were standing here right now. That is who we are playing for today. This game, and every game after this one, are the most important of our lives so far. We will not play with our heads hanging low and our feet dragging along the ground. We will play the way Felix played every match—with focus, might, and joy."

As Georges spoke, the children slowly lifted their heads. Hettie dried her eyes, Greta's sniffles faded, and color returned to Peter's cheeks.

"Now," Georges said. "Shall we walk to the pitch?"

Sophia and Hettie led the group. Georges, Elka and Ziggy brought up the rear. Elka was tempted to turn around and take one last look at Darcy and Francois, but why add to her roller coaster of feelings? Still, her heart ached thinking she would never see either of them again.

"This is so strange," Ziggy told her.

"I know," Elka agreed. "Do you have the shawl?"

Ziggy nodded and patted his hip. She could make out an extra layer beneath his shirt, tucked into the waistband of his blue trousers. She felt peaceful, knowing they would have her father's—no, their fathers'—tallis with them today.

"Do you have the medal?"

"Yes." The gold medal Felix had given her jiggled in her pocket. Today, she would win the race to escape.

As they rounded another corner, the talk quieted, then stopped. Elka stood on tiptoe, trying to see around Georges. Her stomach dropped.

"Ziggy. Look."

Two guards, Nazi soldiers, paced a block ahead. Georges turned around and walked backwards, facing the children.

"Smiles, now!" he said. "We're almost to the field!"

Elka swiftly obeyed, but boy, this felt awkward. She must've looked ridiculous. The other children wore happy faces, too. All of them—except Peter.

He'd stopped walking altogether, like his feet were glued to the cobblestones. Elka rushed to step in front of him, to shield the soldiers' view.

She linked the boy's arm in hers. "Peter?"

His entire body quivered. Last night, he'd seen Felix snatched away. How could he stroll past these soldiers like nothing was wrong?

Suddenly, a wave of panic overcame her. Their entire plan was doomed. What was Georges thinking? Why had she believed they could pull this off? Could she leave the others here, in Annemasse? Peter was about to have a meltdown, which would draw the guards' attention, and then Greta would surely cry. Within seconds, everything would come undone.

No. Elka shook her head. She'd made the mistake of allowing this thought before, in the woods behind the chateau, the night the gendarmes came to raid them. They'd survived! A vivid image of Marcel, finger pressed to his lips, formed in her mind. Without another thought, she mimicked him.

Peter stared at her; his head cocked to one side. His breathing evened out, though his face was pained. The other children stopped walking, too. They turned to watch her theatrics.

Placing her hands on her hips, she defiantly faced the street. She took a step forward, then leaped back in mock surprise, clutching her nose as if she'd been smacked with a rake handle. A snort escaped Peter. He clapped his hands over his mouth to smother the noise.

Elka looked over at Ziggy, and he nodded. Then he spun around and slapped the air with his hands as if stuck inside an unseen box. After his exaggerated exit from the invisible trap, Elka pretended to lasso a rope around Peter's waist. She gave him a hard "tug". Thankfully it worked: Peter lunged forward, laughing, as she "pulled" him down the street. They cheerfully passed the soldiers, who gave them a hasty glance, then waved at Georges. Georges saluted back, and soon the children were at the end of the street and the guards were out of sight.

Her palms sweating, Elka handed Peter the invisible rope. He began to chase a shrieking Greta, twirling the imaginary lasso over his head.

"Good thinking," Ziggy whispered, and Elka managed a brave smile.

"Here we are!" Georges announced. She looked at the soccer pitch, at the swaying oaks that lined it like a crowd of spectators. Goalposts stood on both ends, their nets rippling. The wind was in their favor. They'd made it this far, to the field.

She was about to play the game of her life.

19

Ziggy

On the far side, storm clouds rested above the Alps like gray, sleeping giants. A short distance uphill, automobiles rumbled, and here and there, families flew dragon-tailed kites in the park.

For the hundredth time, Ziggy touched his hip. Since Elka had shown him the tallis, everything seemed surreal. The smooth, carefully folded fabric pressed against his waistband like a secret promise.

It was a dreamlike scene—except for the uniformed guards.

"Okay, everyone!" Georges called out brightly. "Ready for the big game?"

The children stormed the field. Amidst their thunderous energy, a peacefulness he'd never experienced settled over Ziggy. His mind ping-ponged back and forth, but his nerves were steady. This was going to work. This was never going to work. Whatever happened, he would be ready for it. He had to be.

Georges blew his whistle, and the game began.

Ziggy tended goal. Elka was their team's midfielder. On the opposing team, Sophia—who'd grown two inches taller since the Sports Festival—played center forward. She'd filled Felix's position, dribbling the ball with grace and speed. But each time he looked at her, all Ziggy could think was Felix belonged here, tricking the soldiers with his misdirected kicks, and then escaping across the border.

Pay attention, he scolded himself. Elka marked Sophia, then Ziggy spied Hettie positioning for a pass. Sure enough, Sophia dribbled around Elka, straight toward Hettie. Ziggy braced himself as Hettie took aim and kicked.

He lunged to the left, arms high over his head, and the ball slapped his palms. His teammates erupted. He tossed the ball to Elka. She trapped it by dropping the ball to her feet, then passed it back to Ziggy who sent it downfield. But it was stolen by Sophia—her long legs were too much for Peter's clumsy footwork.

Ziggy laughed. The weight of the night before lifted for one exquisite moment, like this was a normal soccer game.

The older kids were sweat soaked when Georges called for half-time. He handed off cups of water, one-by-one. While the smaller children took a rest from the intense heat, he motioned for Ziggy and Elka. Ziggy drained his cup, wishing he could guzzle at least ten more, then hop-skipped to the sideline.

"Great job today, both of you," Georges said in a low voice. "Let's do one or two more plays before going for the win, okay?"

Ziggy nodded. "Yes, sir."

"Yes, sir," Elka repeated.

"You're ready for this, I promise you. Just follow the tree markers," Georges said. "Because of the example you've set, the others will be ready, too." He paused. "I want you both to know how proud I am of you."

Suddenly, Ziggy realized this was goodbye. He'd known it all along, but it was like the wind was knocked out of him. "I'm forever grateful, Monsieur," he said, quickly wiping his eyes.

For a moment, Elka looked like she might throw her arms around Georges' waist. Then she glanced at the bustling avenue and seemed to think better of it. "Thank you for…for everything," she said.

He smiled at them, then toward the field. He lifted his whistle and the shrill blast sent the children scurrying back.

Ziggy's gaze met Elka's. Her eyes looked tortured, like there was a tornado inside her.

He moved closer—their shoulders touching, so no one else could hear. "What's wrong? It's time for us to go. Georges is counting on us."

Her breath hitched. "I can't do it. I can't leave the others." She covered her face with her hands. "I can't do it again."

Ziggy squeezed her shoulder. "Look at me."

Elka lifted her hands from her face. It was streaked with dirt and tears.

"The night when you last saw Ruth—that was four years ago. You were eight years old. It wasn't your fault. You need to know that. You need to forgive yourself."

"But—"

"Do you trust Georges?"

"Yes."

"I do, too," Ziggy pleaded. "He said if we play the game first, he'll be able to save everyone. I believe him."

She sucked in a deep breath. "I believe him too."

"Ready then?"

Elka adjusted her ponytail. "I think so. Ready."

"Okay. Let's show them how to do this."

Ziggy took his place—*Felix's* place—as center forward. It wasn't a position he would usually play, since center forwards do a lot of running. But if everything went according to plan, he would only be playing a few minutes.

Georges blew his whistle again to start the game. Ziggy controlled the ball, passing to Peter. The boy aimed a kick straight at the goal. Hettie caught it, but Ziggy and his teammates celebrated for Peter anyway.

"Your shooting has improved so much!" Elka told him. Peter beamed.

Sophia passed the ball down the pitch, but Elka stole it before David could defend the play. Ziggy watched as she drove it up field, tapping it with the insides of her feet, then pretending to set up a winning kick.

"*Aww!*"

The ball went sailing far off to the left—right over Ziggy's head, into the forest. Elka faked a pout. It was so convincing, Ziggy almost laughed.

"I'll get it!" he called out, loping unevenly off the field.

The entire world hushed at once. The automobiles, the chirping of birds, even the breeze—everything muted. Ziggy stopped himself from checking over his shoulder. Was Greta watching him go, holding in her laughter? Was Peter okay?

And the soldiers on the street—were they watching?

He wouldn't look back. He held his breath as he half-limped, half-ran, ignoring the throbbing in his leg. He stared at the spot where the ball disappeared. He was so fixated on the tree line he didn't see the fat root sticking out of the ground until it was too late.

"*Ah!*" An agonized cry escaped his lips as he fell. Pain ripped through his left ankle, radiating up his calf. Ziggy landed hard on the dry grass; his foot hooked around the traitorous root. He rolled onto his back and wiggled it free, but he could see his ankle swelling. Sprained, maybe broken.

All eyes turned to him. Elka, the other children, Georges…and on the street, two Nazis stopped to have a word with one another at the edge of the field. They hadn't seen him lying there—not yet—but with everyone staring at him, it was simply a matter of time.

It was all over.

20

Elka

Elka stayed in position, save for her heart sinking like a stone. She saw Ziggy stumble and fall, saw the unnatural turn of his ankle, the way he writhed in pain. This couldn't be happening. Not when they were so close.

Then she looked across the field at Georges. He was already jogging—not toward Ziggy, but to the street, where the two Nazis were talking. As the game came to a standstill and the children fell silent, the men looked over.

Georges lifted a hand to them, in a friendly gesture. As he did, he shot a glance at Elka and mouthed a single word so fast, she almost missed it.

Go.

"Good afternoon, gentlemen!" Georges' voice rang out. He hurried over to greet the guards. "Lovely day for a game, isn't it?"

Elka ran off the field, Hettie right on her heels. Looking over her shoulder, she saw Hettie grab the spare ball on the sideline.

"Let's go, team!" she called out. "This game's not over yet!"

Elka practically exploded with admiration for Hettie. Already, she was stepping up and taking charge of the younger ones. As the game resumed, Elka reached Ziggy, lying on the ground. She knelt at his side. His face was alabaster, his lips a thin line. Purple bloomed over the skin on his ankle. His whole foot contorted at an awkward angle.

"This is our shot," she whispered, holding her hands out. But even before Ziggy spoke, she knew what he was about to say. It was written all over his face.

"I can't walk. There's no way I can run. You escape! It's over for me."

Then a flicker caught her eye. A shadow flitted through the trees, and she swore someone was watching her.

Not just anyone. Her sister.

Something clicked inside her then. Way down deep, in that quietest, most secret, and hidden place. A waiting sort of feeling, like a caterpillar wrapped in its cocoon before it becomes a butterfly. Waiting for a second chance, an opportunity to set things right. All those months, she chased Ruth through the woods, hoping to catch her and undo that terrible night four years ago when she'd fled and left her little sister behind.

Elka stood and held out her hands.

"Get up," she told Ziggy. "I'm going to carry you."

21

Ziggy

Ziggy looked at Elka in disbelief. He must have heard her wrong.

"Carry me?"

The wind whipped her ponytail. Stray pieces of hair clung to her neck; her eyes blazed. She didn't lower her hands. "Get up, Zig."

"I'll slow you down," he repeated. "Just—"

"It's good to offer help," she cut in. "But better to accept it. If everyone turned down help when they needed it, there wouldn't be any point. Isn't that what your pa said?"

Just then, Ziggy wasn't sure whether to laugh or cry. "But how can you *carry* me?"

"On my back. Like I used to carry Ruth when we played piggy-back."

He stared up at his friend, full of love and frustration in equal measure. She wouldn't leave him behind like she had her sister. Even if none of it had been her fault, the regret was too much to bear. Any second now, the guards talking to Georges would spot the two of them. There'd be no escape for either. Elka would be captured because she was stubborn.

But wasn't he being obstinate, too?

He tried to tell himself he'd prepared for this, for the worst scenario. He gritted his teeth against the agonizing pain in his ankle, felt the prayer shawl shifting beneath his shirt.

Ziggy closed his eyes. *Have faith.*

He saw those two words in his father's neat penmanship. Two words that for the past four years had filled him with despair, anger, resentment…and hope. And last night, he'd felt real faith; he'd felt his father's presence. He'd allowed himself to embrace it, and he wasn't ready to give it up.

Ziggy didn't want to accept his fate. He wanted to survive.

Survival meant accepting help.

Opening his eyes, he reached out and grabbed Elka's hands.

"Let's go."

22

Elka

Ziggy skittered on one foot, with Elka supporting him, until they were in the forest, out of view. She could hear the game going on behind her. He scrambled clumsily onto her back. The shadow was up ahead, waiting for the race to begin.

This time, she was going to win.

Elka shot ahead like an arrow, squeezing the underside of Ziggy's knees, his arms tight around her collarbone. Some part of her brain registered his weight, but the adrenaline pulsating through her veins was so strong he might as well have been a feather. Elka charged through the woods, her eyes never leaving the shadow of her sister. It flew faster and faster.

Time pulled and pushed. Elka ran for an hour… or maybe just half a minute. The pounding in her ears drowned out all other sounds: the game, Ziggy's breathing, the Nazis who might very well be giving chase right now. She didn't look back to check. She stayed focused on Ruth, on driving forward, on escaping.

When the shadow leapt from behind a tree, she gasped.

Marcel stood there, finger to his lips. Elka's legs trembled and she lost her grip on Ziggy.

Swiftly, Marcel swooped him up, slinging him over one shoulder like a sack of rice. Without a word, he took her hand, interlocking his rough, warm fingers. He squeezed, and looked at her with an expression that said, *ready?*

Then they ran.

Without Ziggy on her back, Elka was wing-footed. She floated over branches, roots, and rocks. Just when she thought they'd be running forever—and maybe she'd be okay with that—they reached a fence.

Elka stopped, out of breath—and stared. The barbed wire in front of her had sharp points lining the top like wolf fangs. Even though the woods on the other side looked the same, Elka knew they were worlds apart.

They were steps away from freedom.

On the other side, a young woman stepped out from behind a tree. She and Marcel locked eyes a moment.

Then Marcel set Ziggy gently on the ground and pulled a piece of duck cloth from his pocket. He wrapped it around the barbed wires and pulled them apart, just wide enough for a child to wriggle through. He and Elka helped Ziggy hobble toward the fence.

"Thank you," Ziggy whispered to Marcel, who smiled.

Once Ziggy was through, Elka turned to Marcel.

"Thank you." Her voice cracked, and her legs threatened to give way. But when Marcel took her hand one last time, her strength returned.

"You're welcome," he whispered back.

Elka slipped through the fence. When she straightened up, she saw Ziggy leaning on the young woman's shoulder. His face was still pale, but his eyes sparkled. Elka looked from him to the woman, who had honey-colored hair pulled into a bun. She wore red lipstick, just like Mademoiselle Bellegard.

The young woman smiled at Elka.

"Welcome to Switzerland," she said softly.

Two kilometers away, the soccer match ended. The next week, there was another game, and then another, and another. One by one, more children chased the ball into the woods. Every time someone shimmed through the barbed wire, the team celebrated a goal.

Their soaring cheers rang in the soldiers' ears.

EPILOGUE

May 1945

Elka sat at her mahogany desk, feet crossed at the ankles under her chair. Three equations left to solve, and then Marianne would permit her to go on a quick run by the lake before dinner.

Marianne and Vincent Baumann had been Elka and Ziggy's foster parents for nearly a year now. They were as kind as they were wealthy—Elka still hadn't grown accustomed to life with servants and brand-new dresses and so many pillows on her bed. She tossed a few on the floor every night before climbing in.

After arriving in Switzerland, Elka and Ziggy were taken to a reception camp for a few days before being sent to a children's home in Geneva. The place was clean, and food was plentiful. She was ecstatic when Hettie arrived the following week, followed by Sophia, who told them a game of catch with Georges had allowed her escape. When he tossed the ball a little too hard, she ducked into the woods and disappeared.

Over the next year, every single child from their chateau and others, too—whether they climbed the cemetery wall or chased a soccer ball—made it safely to Switzerland. All thanks to Georges Loinger.

And they weren't the only ones. Marianne volunteered for the Swiss Red Cross, and she kept Elka and Ziggy informed on the rescue efforts of the OSE. Thousands of Jewish orphans from Holland, Belgium, and Italy had also made it into Switzerland. Some of the luckier ones had celebrated tear-filled reunions with their families.

Elka took that tidbit of information and tucked it away in the most sacred corner of her heart. Neither she nor Ziggy ever received a letter from their parents. As a year passed, and then another, Elka's memories of Mama and Papa became distant, more dream-like, slipping from her mind like flour through a sieve.

But her memory of Ruth was clearer than ever.

Downstairs, Elka could hear Ziggy—who'd finished his homework an hour before Elka, as usual—speaking to Marianne in the kitchen. His voice was deep now, almost as low as Vincent's, and sometimes when he spoke, a bunch of odd emotions would shiver deep in Elka's gut. Some of those emotions, she couldn't identify. But the strongest was easy to name, because it lived with her for so long, it was almost an old friend: fear.

Six months ago, Elka and Ziggy learned that a boy named Abe whom they'd befriended at the children's home in Geneva, had been forced to return to France. He'd turned sixteen, and since he was no longer considered a child, Swiss authorities weren't obligated to protect him. Both Elka and Ziggy were months from turning sixteen, so Abe's story horrified them. And while Elka couldn't imagine kind Marianne and Vincent making them leave, she couldn't shake the dread that grew a little stronger with every passing day.

Even the small possibility of being sent back to France alone, where they'd almost certainly be consigned to the camps, was terrifying.

The thought of it seared her insides. She dropped her pencil.

"Elka!"

Ziggy's voice rose an octave, and there was an urgency in his tone that sent her pulse racing.

Elka leaped down the stairs two at a time, sliding her hand along the polished banister. She skidded across the waxed hardwood floor in the foyer and burst into the kitchen.

Ziggy and Marianne were standing at the table, their eyes locked on the radio. Marianne wiped her hands on her apron; behind her, Elka saw a ball of dough and a pile of cherries on the counter next to the sink, but even the thought of cherry strudel couldn't quell the panic rising in her chest.

Ziggy ran a hand over his head, a habit he'd developed ever since shearing his thick brown locks earlier that spring. The haircut made his dark eyes seem even larger, his cheekbones sharper. He was taller than her now, although the custom-made shoes Marianne and Vincent supplied him deserved some of the credit for that.

"Churchill is expected to make an announcement," he told Elka. He kept a serious expression, but his eyes sparkled. Elka placed a hand to her stomach as butterflies fluttered. She moved closer as Marianne turned the volume dial up on the radio. A few seconds later, the familiar voice of the Prime Minister of the United Kingdom crackled through the airwaves and filled the warm kitchen.

Buzzing filled Elka's ears at the word surrender, growing to a drone that drowned out Churchill's words. But she'd heard enough of them to know what miracle was happening: "*Yesterday morning at two forty-one a.m. at General Eisenhower's headquarters, General Jodl, the representative of the German high command and of Grand Admiral Donitz, the designated head of the German state, signed the act of unconditional surrender of all German land, sea and air forces in Europe to the Allied expeditionary force…*"

Marianne's hands flew up and color crept into her face. As the broadcast ended, a single tear trickled down her flushed cheek.

"It's over," she whispered. "It's truly over."

Something swelled inside Elka. Excitement so fierce and powerful, it couldn't be contained, couldn't be still. Without thinking, she ran from the kitchen and out of the house.

Elka pulled her hair bun loose and sprinted across the lawn. She slowed enough for Ziggy to catch up, then took his hand and the two ran down the brick road. Cries and cheers came from the houses around them, and here and there, more people began to spill out of their homes and onto the streets, all with the same looks of elation and disbelief, as if they all thought they'd imagined Churchill's words and needed to see whether anyone else heard them, too.

Elka and Ziggy didn't slow until they reached downtown. Already, the scene was that of an impromptu parade; people dancing in the streets, hugging, crying, laughing. Ziggy kept hold of Elka's hand as they stood in the center of it all, too overwhelmed to even speak.

As the crowd grew thicker, the back of Elka's neck prickled. She closed her eyes and, for a moment, she was back in the woods behind the chateau, running along the path in the dark, chasing a shadow. Only now, for the first time, Elka realized the shadow had never been running away from her.

It had been leading her to this, here, right now.

Elka opened her eyes. Through the throng of people ahead, a girl stood facing west. She was familiar yet unfamiliar, a willowy five-foot-tall, but still a few years younger than Elka. She held a suitcase in one hand and looked at a letter in the other. Her skirt, decorated with tiny, embroidered birds was rumpled, as though she'd traveled a long distance.

The girl's profile sent a spark zipping through Elka. Someone she knew from the chateau, perhaps Greta or one of the other little ones, Elka told herself—even as her heart began singing a different melody.

"Ziggy," Elka managed to say. She needed him to see this, because if he didn't witness it, it might not be real. "Ziggy, look." She pointed with her free hand, which trembled.

Next to her, Ziggy turned and saw the girl. "She looks like you," he said in surprise. "She looks just like you the day we met."

That was all Elka needed to hear. As if the girl sensed her stare, she turned, and their eyes locked. Her lips parted in a soft, surprised O, her hand fluttering to her throat in a gesture so like Mama it brought all those memories Elka thought she'd lost rushing back like a tidal wave.

"Ruth," Elka whispered, and then she was running, running as fast as she could toward her sister.

Author's Note

As with the prayer shawl Elka gave Ziggy, we all have a personal tapestry. Every stitch and colorful thread contain stories of resilience that connect us in unexpected ways.

Freedom's Game was inspired by Georges Loinger's fierce resolve in the face of despair. I first saw his captivating smile in a newspaper photo, 13 years before he passed away at age 108. In the picture, he was humbly accepting a gold medallion in Paris. Reading a passage about Georges' heroics made me determined to learn more. This book is a work of fiction, based on real events in his valiant life, told through the eyes of two 12-year-olds.

Organized protests like the famous Warsaw Uprising show Jewish people resisted the Hitler regime. In fact, there were countless other courageous, less-publicized acts by Jews that historical accounts overlook. I'm grateful for members of the Jewish French Resistance like Georges, who were often very young—and unafraid. They took great risks to save thousands of lives; danger lurked with their every attempt to usher children to safety.

I'm also grateful for my Jewish upbringing and ancestry—the inspiration for my two brave protagonists, Elka and Ziggy. My maternal grandmother, Flora, grew up in a small German town called Gemunden. Her parents worked as cattle drivers, but they would ensure their children got a good education. In 1911, Flora and her younger brother Louis—who became a leading sociologist at the University of Chicago—sailed by ship to America, to attend school. Eventually, their four other siblings arrived, too.

Years later, my grandma graduated from college with an English Literature degree and became a teacher. And Louis sponsored many family members immigrating to the United States, to escape economic hardship and the rising tide of anti-Semitism in their home country.

Things took a dark turn in Germany in 1933, 15 years after World War I ended. A struggling German government granted Adolf Hitler the powers of a dictator. Three days later, Hitler outlined anti-Jewish measures, such as boycotts against Jewish stores and businesses. Graffiti and signs on Jewish-owned store windows warned shoppers not to buy from them. Those who didn't go along with Hitler's rules were harassed.

On the night of November 9, 1938, Nazi leaders coordinated a violent attack on Jews in Germany. Now known as the November Pogrom—and widely referred to as Kristallnacht, or "Night of the Broken Glass"—they torched synagogues and smashed the windows of Jewish homes and storefronts. Then, in September of 1939, Hitler's invasion of Poland spurred France to declare war on Germany. The German military's style of warfare, known as the Blitzkreig, decimated France's defenses. On June 22, 1940, Nazi troops captured the northern half of the country. Soon, Jews in France, as in other parts of Nazi-occupied Europe were ordered to wear yellow stars. These badges foreshadowed the mass deportations to follow.

In 1943, exiled French leader Charles de Gaulle helped organize the Resistance, a group of undercover fighters that had reached 10,000 in number by war's end. Resistance fighters did more than smuggle children to safety. They also attacked key intelligence and transportation targets, and intercepted harmful Nazi propaganda.

The southern part of France, nicknamed the Free Zone, made the city of Vichy its capital. However, the nickname was misleading since the Vichy government helped the Nazi party shuttle Jewish citizens to Germany's concentration camps. In France, between 1942 and 1944, over 75,000 Jews were rounded up this way. 11,000 of them were children. They were later deported to Nazi concentration camps like Auschwitz. Only a tiny percentage survived.

In all, a quarter of France's Jewish population was wiped out. Likewise, many of my own relatives who stayed in

Germany perished in concentration camps. When the Allies invaded Paris in 1944, the last train deporting Jews left for Germany.

Two million French soldiers were captured by Nazis. Among them was Georges Loinger. He was arrested and sent to a prisoner-of-war camp near Munich. Using his fluent German and fair coloring as decoys, Georges managed to flee the camp and join the French Resistance. His wife, Flore, was working with the Oeuvre Secours aux Enfants (OSE), an aid society for Jewish children supported by the Resistance. By 1941, the OSE had moved colonies of kids to isolated mansions (chateaux) in southern France. These children's homes set up by the OSE acted as sanctuaries for children in hiding. The Chateau de Chabannes was one of these— a French safe house for Jewish children fleeing persecution.

After joining the Resistance, Georges was picked to spearhead their efforts. When Nazis boarded a train of Jewish refugee children in his care, Georges' quick thinking hid the kids' identities. He also knew the mayor of Annemasse, a French village only a few miles from Geneva, Switzerland. Mayor Jean Deffaugt owned a men's clothing store where he and Georges devised a plan to protect the children; Deffaugt allowed Georges to bring the children to Annemasse until it was time for their escape. In 1965, Israel's official Holocaust memorial, Yad Vashem, honored Mayor Deffaugt as

"Righteous Among Nations" for his role in saving Jewish children during the war. Many non-Jews, like Deffaugt, played a crucial part in these rescues. For instance, Felix Chevrier, the real-life director of Chateau de Chabannes, intentionally misread the kids' names during a police raid. (Felix in *Freedom's Game* is named in his honor.)

The children understood the need to hide their identity. Thanks to Resistance members skilled in forging false paperwork, they adopted new names and religions—disposing of anything that seemed Jewish or foreign. Like Mademoiselle Bellegard, the Paillassou sisters—devoted teachers at Chateau de Chabannes—really did risk everything by refusing to bring Jewish students to a rally for Philippe Petain. And what about Frau Wagner, who took in Ziggy and his mother? There were many good people like her, who boldly hid Jews in their homes. Most know the true story of Anne Frank and the individuals who sheltered her family in the Secret Annex. There were others who did the same, even though the consequences for doing this kind of work were perilous.

To attempt escape, Georges knew the young refugees must be physically strong. Using his knowledge of athletics to run "sports camps"—which on at least one occasion included a Sports Festival—Georges devised clever ways to deliver the children into neutral territory. Because they were in danger of immediate deportation, older children were often smuggled out first. Not just soccer matches, but also games of catch were played with getaways in mind. The cemetery scene, too, was an actual ruse Georges used to shuttle children to Switzerland. Imagine what these children endured! Not only were their living conditions extremely difficult, but most were orphans, grappling with the pain of losing their parents. Add to that their constant fear of capture. Yet they still climbed walls and snuck past guards. These kids had incredible guts!

Of the many tactics Georges used, one involved the famous Jewish mime, Marcel Marceau. (Marcel's real last name was Mangel; using the French surname Marceau helped him remain undiscovered.) The men were first cousins, and Georges tapped Marcel's talents to keep the kids calm and quiet. Miming allowed the children to communicate in silence while they were smuggled over borders. To trick the authorities, sometimes they pretended to be going on vacation. Other times, the actor posed as a Boy Scout leader taking kids for a hike. Once they reached Switzerland, someone else would take them to shelter.

Georges Loinger continued his acts of courage until France was liberated from Nazi occupation in 1944. Altogether, he saved the lives of more than 400 children. Even after the war, he helped displaced people find homes abroad. In 2005, Georges was granted the Legion of Honour, France's highest military and civil merit award—the medal he's receiving in the photograph when we first "met."

Acknowledgements

Where to start? I'm thankful for so much, and to so many.

The highlight reel:

Much love and gratitude to my best friend and bashert, Hal. Thank you for believing in this book, and in me. To my children—Josie, Jack, Danny, and AJ—I lucked out with all of you. If any of you grew tired of listening to me read earlier versions of *Freedom's Game* aloud, for the hundredth time, I'm grateful you didn't show it. Seriously. My heart is full.

My deepest thanks to Sunita Apte, my acquiring editor, for knowing exactly what I wanted this book to be, and for taking such loving care of Elka and Ziggy; and to the amazing team at Reycraft—many thanks for the hours of hard work that went into creating this title. It definitely takes a village. My appreciation and admiration to my editor Jeff Fuerst, for his feedback and advice (even after retirement!), and to my extraordinary critique partner (and dear friend) Christina Vagenius. To Vali Mintzi, the cover of this book couldn't be more beautiful. Thank you for sharing your incredible talent.

Many non-fiction books, articles, and interviews inspired me to write this novel, but I especially want to acknowledge those that were most influential. My invaluable sources included: The United States Holocaust Museum's "Oral History with Georges Loinger"; Yad Vashem's "Video Testimonials of Children's Homes in France During the Holocaust"; Director Lisa Gosell's spectacularly important documentary film *The Children of Chabannes*, co-directed by Dean Wetherell (Good Egg Productions, 2000), and *The Children of La Hille*, written by Walter W. Reed.

These stories of resistance and survival can never be told enough.

Additional thanks to Catriella Freedman and all the folks at PJ Our Way and the Harold Grinspoon Foundation, for encouraging earlier drafts of this work with an author incentive grant. The boost you've given to contemporary Jewish children's literature is immeasurable. To Alvin Rosenfeld, Professor of English and Jewish Studies at Indiana University-Bloomington, thank you (thank you!) for promptly responding to my emails amid a busy college semester. Your Literature of the Holocaust class was always my favorite. Many thanks to Muriel Madden, my wonderful, soft-spoken seventh-grade creative writing teacher at Parkway Central Junior High for encouraging me to express myself with poetry during the awkward years; and to Dennis Aron, whose dedication to tracing our family tree (with detailed accounts of nearly 100 shared family members who died in Nazi concentration camps) shaped many pieces of this book. Your genealogy research and reference documents are a priceless resource for future generations, and an important reminder to never forget. L'dor v'dor.

And where would I be without my amazing sisters, Flora Dulle, Allison Creighton, and Jennifer Grasser— you guys are my compass when life gets messy. Thank you to my extraordinary aunt, Claudia Horn, for your unconditional love, and to Kim Selig for your forever friendship and bright spirit. You're like family to me. Many thanks to my paternal grandmother, Frances Gellman, from whom I learned many things, including that it's never too late to create works of art. To my mother-in-law Babe Tolin, the same can be said of you; many thanks for loving our family so fiercely.

To my Uncle Larry Joseph, Professor Emeritus of French Language and Literature at Smith College, thank you for being my window into the Wirths.

Thank you to my dad, Dr. Elliot Gellman, for passing on your passion for Holocaust history. It's my humblest hope that your legacy lives on, just a little bit, on these pages. To my mother, Joann Gellman, I love you for hanging my very first poems on the refrigerator door like they were masterpieces. Much of this book was made in your memory. Mom and Dad, I miss you both so much.

And last (but not at all least), a shiny gold star to my genius agent Elizabeth Copps, for championing *Freedom's Game* from the very beginning. The publishing journey is hard, and I'm grateful you're running alongside me.

About the Author

Born and raised in St. Louis, MO, Rosanne Tolin is the author of *More Than Marmalade: Michael Bond and The Story Of Paddington Bear* and *Freedom's Game*. An experienced and respected journalist, her work has focused primarily on children's publications. She was the creator of an ALA notable website for kids, the managing editor of a children's magazine, and a Hoosier State Press Award-winning features writer. She lives in Chesterton, Indiana with her husband. When not working, she can be found hiking with her dogs in the Indiana Dunes or Colorado's Tenmile Range.